MONROE COLLEGE LIBRARY

3 7340 01084249 7

OCTAVIA E. BUTLER

PATTERN-MASTER

WARNER BOOKS

A Time Warner Company

PS
3552
.U845
P38
1995

If you purchase this book without a cover you should be aware that this book may have been stolen property and reported as "unsold and destroyed" to the publisher. In such case neither the author nor the publisher has received any payment for this "stripped book."

WARNER BOOKS EDITION

Copyright © 1976 by Octavia E. Butler
All rights reserved.

Aspect is a trademark of Warner Books, Inc.

This Warner Books Edition is published by arrangement with the author.

Cover design by Don Puckey
Cover illustration by John Jude Palencar
Hand lettering By Ron Zin

Warner Books, Inc.
1271 Avenue of the Americas
New York, NY 10020

Visit our web site at
http://pathfinder.com/twep

Ⓦ A Time Warner Company

Printed in the United States of America

First Warner Books Printing: May, 1995

10 9 8 7 6 5 4 3 2

▪ Prologue ▪

Rayal had his lead wife, Jansee, with him on that last night. He lay beside her in his huge bed, secure, lulled by the peacefulness of the Pattern as it flowed to him. The Pattern had been peaceful for over a year now. A year without a major Clayark attack on any sector of Patternist Territory. A luxury. Rayal had known enough years of fighting to be glad to relax and enjoy the respite. Only Jansee could still find reason for discontent. Her children, as usual.

"I think tomorrow I'll send a mute to check on our sons," she said.

Rayal yawned. He found her too much like a mute herself in her concern for her young. The two boys, aged twelve and two, were at school in Redhill Sector, 480 kilometers away. She would have gone against custom and kept them near her at the school in Forsyth, their birth sector, if he had let her. "Why bother?" he said. "You're linked with them. If there was anything wrong with them, you would be the first to realize it. Why send a mute to find out what you already know?"

"Because I'll be able to see them through the mute's memory when he comes back. I haven't seen either of

1

them for over two years. Not since the youngest was born."

Rayal shook his head. "Why do you want to see them?"

"I don't know. There's something . . . not wrong, but . . . I don't know." He could feel her uneasiness influencing the Pattern, rippling its vast interwoven surface. "Will you let me send a mute?"

"Send an outsider. He'll be better able to defend himself if the Clayarks notice him." Then he smiled. "You should have more children. Perhaps then you would be less concerned for these two." She was used to his mocking. He had said such things to her before. But this time she seemed to take him seriously. He could feel her attention on him, focused, aware even of his smile, though she could not see him in the darkness.

"You want me to have children by one of your outsiders?" she asked.

He looked toward her in surprise, his mind tracing the solemnity of her expression. She was calling his bluff. She should have known better. "By a journeyman, perhaps."

"What?"

"Have them by a journeyman, or at least an apprentice. Not an outsider."

"And which . . . journeyman or apprentice did you have in mind?"

He turned away from her in annoyance. She was continuing this nonsense to goad him. No other woman in his House would dare to bait him so. Perhaps, for a change, she should not be allowed to get away with it either.

"Michael will do," he said quietly.

HIGHEST PRAISE FOR OCTAVIA E. BUTLER

◆

"Butler's books are exceptional. . . . Butler is a realist, writing the most detailed social criticism and creating some of the most fascinating female characters in the genre . . . the hard edge of cruelty, violence, and domination is described in stark detail . . . real women caught in impossible situations."
—*Village Voice*

◆

"Butler's spare, vivid prose style invites comparison with the likes of Kate Wilhelm and Ursula Le Guin."—*Kirkus Reviews*

◆

"A new Octavia Butler novel is an exciting event. . . . She is one of those rare authors who pay serious attention to the way human beings actually work together and against each other, and she does so with extraordinary plausibility."   —*Locus*

◆

"Butler sets the imagination free, blending the real and the possible."   —**United Press International**

◆

"Butler's exploration of people is clear-headed and brutally unsentimental. . . . If you haven't read Butler, you don't yet understand how rich the possibilities of science fiction can be."   —*The Magazine of Fantasy & Science Fiction*

◆

"Butler's strength is her ability to create complete and believable characters."   —*San Francisco Chronicle*

◆

"Butler is among the best of contemporary SF writers, blessed with a mind capable of conceiving complicated futuristic situations that shed considerable light on our current affairs. Her prose is lean and literate, her ideas expansive and elegant."
—*Houston Post*

◆

"Her books are disturbing, unsettling . . . her visions are strange, hypnotic distortions of our own uncomfortable world. . . . Butler's African-American feminist perspective is unique, and uniquely suited to reshape the boundaries of the genre."   —*LA Style*

Books by Octavia E. Butler

ADULTHOOD RITES
CLAY'S ARK
DAWN
IMAGO
KINDRED
MIND OF MY MIND
PATTERNMASTER
SURVIVOR
WILD SEED
PARABLE OF THE SOWER

ATTENTION: SCHOOLS AND CORPORATIONS
WARNER books are available at quantity discounts with bulk purchase for educational, business, or sales promotional use. For information, please write to: SPECIAL SALES DEPARTMENT, WARNER BOOKS, 1271 AVENUE OF THE AMERICAS, NEW YORK, N.Y. 10020

"Mich . . . Rayal!" He enjoyed the indignation in her voice. Michael was a young apprentice just out of school and about ten years Jansee's junior.

"You asked me to choose someone for you. I've chosen Michael."

She thought about that for a while, then retreated. But her pride did not allow her to retreat far. "Someday when you promote Michael to journeyman and he can hear me without embarrassment, I'm going to tell him about this." She laid a hand alongside his face. "Then, husband, if you still insist that you will give me no more children, I will accept your choice."

This was, he realized, as much a promise as a threat. She meant it. He reached for her, pulled her closer to him. "It's for your own good that I refuse you. You're really too much the mute-mother to have more children. You care too much what happens to them."

"I care."

"And they're going to kill each other. You're so strong that even your child by a weaker man might be able to compete with our two sons."

"They wouldn't *have* to kill each other."

He gave a mental shrug. "Didn't I have to kill two brothers and a sister to get where I am? Won't at least some of my children and yours be as eager to inherit power as I was?" He felt her try to pull away from him and knew that he had won a point. He held her where she was. "Two brothers and a sister," he repeated. "And it could easily have been two sisters if my strongest sister had not been wise enough to ally herself with me and become my lead wife."

Now he let her go, but she lay still where she was. The Pattern rippled with her sorrow. It reflected her emotions almost as readily as it did his own. But unless he cooperated, it would not respond to her control. He spoke again to her gently.

"Even our sons will compete with each other. That will be difficult enough for you to watch, if it happens during your lifetime."

"But what about your other children," she said. "You have so many by other wives."

"And I'll have more. I don't have your sensitivity. Those of my children who don't compete to succeed me will live to contribute to the people's strength."

She was silent for a long while, her awareness focused on his face. "Would you really have tried to kill me if I had opposed you or refused you?"

"Of course. On your own, you might have become a threat to me."

There was more silence, then, "Do you know why I allied with you instead of contesting?"

"Yes. Now I do."

She went on as though she had not heard him. "I hate killing. We have to kill Clayarks just to survive. I can do that. But we don't have to kill each other."

Rayal jerked the Pattern sharply and Jansee jumped, gasping at the sudden disturbance. It was comparable physically to a painless but startling slap in the face.

"You see?" he said. "I've just awakened several thousand Patternists by exerting no more effort than another person might use to snap his fingers. Sister-wife, that is power worth killing for."

Jansee radiated sudden anger. She thought of her sons fighting and her mind filled with bitter things to say about his power. But the pointlessness of verbalizing them to him, of all people, undermined her anger. "Not to me," she said sadly, "and I hope not to my sons. Let them save their savagery, their power, for the Clayarks." She paused. "Have you noticed the group of mutes outside in front of the House?"

This was not the change of subject that it seemed to be. He knew what she was leading up to but he let her go. "Yes."

"They've come a long way," she said.

"You can let them in if you like."

"I will, later, when they've finished their prayers." She shook her head. "Hajji mutes. Poor fools."

"Jansee . . ."

"They've come here because they think you're a god, and you won't even bother to let them in out of the cold."

"They get exactly what they expect from me, Jansee. The assurance of good health, long life, and protection from abuse by their Masters. Making a religion of their gratitude was their own idea."

"Not that you mind," she said softly. "Power. In fact, since you hold the Pattern, you're even a kind of god to the Patternists, aren't you? Shall I worship you, too, husband?"

"Not that you would." He smiled. "But it doesn't matter. There are times when I need someone around me who isn't afraid of me."

"Lest your own conceit destroy you," she said bitterly.

*   *   *

The Clayarks chose that moment to end the year of peace. With an ancient gun of huge proportions, they stood on a hill just within sight of the lights of Rayal's House. They had found the gun far south in territory that was exclusively their own. With rare patience and fore-thought, they had worked hard with it, cleaning it, coming to understand how it was supposed to work, repairing it, practicing with it. Then they dragged it to the House of the Patternmaster, their greatest enemy. It was unlikely that they would be able to use it more than once. Thus it would be effective only if they could use it against Rayal.

Rayal's sentries noticed them, but, lulled by the peace and unaware of the cannon, they paid no attention to Cla-yarks so far away. Thus the Clayarks had all the time their clumsy fingers needed to load their huge weapon, aim it, and fire.

Their aim was good and they were very lucky. The first shot smashed through the wall of the Patternmaster's pri-vate apartment, beheading the Patternmaster's lead wife and injuring the Patternmaster himself so severely about the head and shoulders that he was totally occupied for long important minutes with saving his own life. For all his power, he lay helpless. The people of his House were surprised enough, disoriented enough, to give the Cla-yarks time to fire again. But the destruction had excited the Clayarks. They abandoned the cannon to swarm down and finish the House in a more satisfying, personal way.

• One •

The sun had not been up long enough to burn off the cold dampness of morning when Teray and Iray left their dormitory room at Redhill School for the last time.

Iray was all eagerness and apprehension and her emotions were contagious. Teray had resigned himself to being caught up in them. The act of leaving the school together not only reinforced their status as adults, but made them husband and wife. Teray had waited four wearisome years for the chance to leave safely and begin working toward his dream of founding his own House.

Now, with Iray, he walked toward the main gate. There was no ceremony—not for their leaving school, nor for their marriage. Only two people paid any attention to their going. Teray sensed them both inside one of the dormitories, a Patternist girl who had been Iray's friend and a middle-aged mute woman. They stood together at a dormitory window, looking down at Iray. The friend kept her feelings to herself, but the mute radiated such a mixture of sadness and excitement that Teray knew she and Iray must have been close.

Iray was too full of her own emotions to be aware of

the pair. Teray flashed her a brief mental image and she reached back, contrite, to say her good-byes.

He sent back no parting thoughts of his own. He had had nothing to do with mutes for years. His maturing mental strength had made him too dangerous to them. For their sakes, he maintained only an impersonal master-servant relationship with them. And he had made few friends among his teachers and fellow students. They too were wary of his strength. He had been a power at the school, but except for Iray he had been much alone.

Outside the main gate, he and Iray met the two men who had been waiting for them. The older man was of medium height and hard, square build, a man of obvious physical strength. The younger man was built more like Teray—tall and lean. He was probably no older than Teray.

Joachim! Teray's thought went out to the older man. *I didn't expect you to come yourself.*

The man smiled faintly and spoke aloud: "It isn't often that I take on such a promising apprentice. I wouldn't want anything to happen to you on your way to my House."

Teray transmitted surprise: *There's been trouble, then? Who was raided?*

"Coransee. And vocalize. I'm spreading my perception as widely as I can just in case the raiders are still in the area."

"Coransee?" said Teray obediently. "So close inside the sector?"

"And the most powerful one of us." The man with

8

Joachim spoke for the first time. "The raiders killed two of his outsiders and kidnaped a mute."

"I hope to heaven they killed the mute too," said Joachim. "Killed him quickly, I mean."

Teray nodded, sharing the hope. Mutes who were not tortured to death and who did not die of the Clayark disease became the worst of their former-masters' enemies. "You think there are still Clayarks inside the sector?" he asked Joachim.

"Yes. That's why I brought Jer along." Joachim gestured toward his companion. "He's one of my strongest outsiders."

Teray glanced at Jer with interest, wondering how the man's strength measured up against his own. Through the Pattern, Teray had already sensed that Jer was strong. But how strong? It was not possible to make a definite determination guided only by the Pattern. No doubt Joachim knew, though. He had probably tested Jer as thoroughly as he had tested Teray. And after the testing, he had made Jer an outsider and accepted Teray as an apprentice.

Iray's voice brought Teray out of his thoughts. "But, Joachim, with both you and Jer here, won't your House be in danger?"

Joachim glanced at her, his grim expression softening. "Not likely. The Clayarks know my reputation. We're all linked in my House. My lead wife can draw strength from everyone in the House for defense. If the Clayarks attack one of my people, the rest know, and they all respond. The Clayarks wouldn't risk attacking them with less than an army, and I don't think they've managed to smuggle an army into the sector."

"We'd have more dead than the larger Houses," said

Jer, "because we don't have their strength. But their people fight as individuals, and we fight as one. Their people always miss some Clayarks and let them escape. We kill them all."

Teray noticed the pride in the man's voice and wondered how Joachim could inspire pride even in an outsider. But then, Teray's attitude toward outsider status was, he knew, colored by his desire never to occupy it. It was a permanently inferior servant position. The best that an outsider could hope for was to find a Housemaster like Joachim whom he could respect and serve with some semblance of pride. The worst he could get was slavery.

The horses waited for them a few steps away in a grove of trees, and Teray noticed that Iray walked the distance beside Joachim. She, who only a few moments before had been so excited about leaving the school with Teray. True, she had known Joachim before she met Teray. The Housemaster had been her second when she made the difficult transition from childhood to adulthood and membership in the Pattern. She would probably have gone into his House as one of his wives if she had not met Teray. Now Teray watched them together with suspicion. He would spend at least two years with Joachim, learning, preparing to begin his own House. If only he did not lose his wife in the process.

He came up beside Iray as they reached the horses. He touched her mind lightly with a one-word reminder carefully screened from Joachim and Jer: *Wife!*

His caution was lost on her. She seized his thought carelessly like a happy child and magnified it to a mental shout. To it, she added enthusiastically, *Husband!*

A proclamation. Joachim and Jer could hardly have missed it. He could feel their amusement as keenly as he could feel his own embarrassment. But at least she had told him what he wanted to know. And, fortunately, she had completely missed his meaning. Of course there was a bond between Iray and Joachim. But it was no more than the bond between any man and a woman he had seconded. Affection. No more.

He cast around for a way to end the silence and focus Joachim's and Jer's attention elsewhere. It was then that he noticed the horse that Joachim had mounted. It was a show horse, of course, as were the three others. They were all as carefully bred and trained as most mutes. They were part of a project that Joachim had undertaken more for enjoyment than profit. But the one Joachim rode was something special.

"Joachim, your horse . . ."

The Housemaster smiled. "I wondered when Iray would let you notice."

Teray let his curiosity be felt partly because he was actually curious, and partly in relief that Joachim too was ignorant of his foolish jealousy. But the horse . . . "You have no mental controls on it at all?"

"None," said Joachim.

Gingerly, Teray felt the stallion out. Gingerly because animals, like mutes, were easily injured, easily killed. And too, uncontrolled animals unconsciously hit intruding Patternist minds with any emotions they felt. Especially violent emotions. But Teray received only calm from the horse. Unusual calm.

"An experiment of mine," said Joachim. "This horse

11

doesn't need to be controlled any more than the average mute. In fact, you program it like a mute. And once it's programmed, the Clayarks could fire a cannon next to it and the programming would hold. You wouldn't have to waste time controlling the horse when you should be giving all your attention to the Clayarks." Joachim grinned. "I'll tell you more about it when we get home."

Teray nodded. Home. Joachim could not know how good that word sounded. The school had been Teray's home for far too long. He had made his transition to adulthood nearly four years before. Even then, there had been little more that the teachers could teach him. But he had stayed, learning what he could about his abilities on his own, getting occasional help from a visiting Housemaster, waiting and hoping for a Housemaster who would accept him as an apprentice.

Several had offered to take him on as an outsider. If he had not still been under the protection of the school, some of them might have been tempted to take him by force. Doubtless that would be possible now, while he was still young and unskilled. And if they took him now, they could prevent him from learning the skills that might make him a danger to them. But no one wanted to risk accepting him as an apprentice. An outsider was a permanent inferior. An apprentice was a potential superior. An apprentice was the young colt hanging around the edges of the herd, biding his time until he could kill off the old herd stallion and take over. Or at least that was the way the Housemasters he had met seemed to feel.

It was much to Joachim's credit that he had not been afraid. In fact, when Iray had introduced Teray to

Joachim, the Housemaster had mentioned the possibility of an apprenticeship before Teray even thought it wise to bring up the matter. It took a confident, powerful Housemaster to accept an apprentice with Teray's potential. But Joachim had had the necessary confidence and power, and now, finally, Teray was going home.

Joachim had taken a lead position with Jer. Now he called back, "We're going to have to stop at Coransee's House first. He wants to see me—probably to get me to help him with his Clayark problem."

Iray caught her breath sharply. "To visit Coransee! Joachim, is he your friend? So powerful a lord." She was a child about half the time.

There was a pause before Joachim answered, then, "I know him." He sounded almost bitter. "We're not friends, but I know him."

As the strongest Housemaster in the sector, Coransee was a kind of unofficial local leader. That made him a celebrity to people like Iray. Teray had heard him spoken of with admiration and envy, but never with bitterness. But then, Teray had been shut away in the school and people were careful what they said before schoolchildren. Well, he was out of school now. It would be best for him to know something more about the Housemaster he was about to visit. "Joachim?" he called.

Joachim dropped back to ride beside Teray, leaving Jer to lead. *You'd better make it "Lord Joachim," Teray. For the rest of the day. And definitely "Lord Coransee." He values formality.*

Teray accepted this with interest. It was the first nonvocal communication he had had with Joachim this morning, and it was nonvocal only to emphasize its seriousness. It was an order, and a warning.

Joachim went on and Teray realized that he was reaching Iray too. *Be introduced to him with Jer and me, then drift away among his women and outsiders.*

"Joachim, what is it?" Iray asked.

Joachim looked at her silently, until she corrected herself.

"Lord Joachim."

"Sector politics," Joachim said aloud. "Nothing more." And he again took his place beside Jer.

Teray watched him, wondering at his sudden reticence. Now Teray had more questions than ever. But Joachim's silence was a closed one. It did not invite questions.

By midday they had reached Coransee's House. It was a four-story mansion, columned, ancient, ornate, surrounded by well-landscaped grounds and flanked by outbuildings. It had been built on a hill and was visible for miles. Teray could see why it was the envy of many lesser lords, and why Coransee had risked fighting a duel for it several years before. To get it, he had had to kill a powerful woman who had held it for over two decades. In school, Teray had seen pictures of ancient palaces that were probably smaller. Teray gazed out over Coransee's land, seeing the side pastures and the grazing horses and cattle. Coransee supplied the sector with most of its meat and its riding animals. The small herd that Joachim kept had never been more than a hobby.

Two mutes hurried from one of the outbuildings to greet the four newcomers politely and take their horses.

As Joachim led the way to the House, he warned Teray and Iray once more:

"Both of you remember what I told you. Take up with a woman, an outsider, even a mute, and get out of the way fast. I'll make it as easy as I can for you."

Teray nodded and Joachim led them inside.

There were several women and outsiders seated and standing near the fireplace of the huge common room in which Teray found himself. Before Teray could decide what they were doing, one of them sent the informing thought, *He knows you're here. He's coming.*

Joachim acknowledged with thanks and sat down. The others followed his example. Their wait was not long.

The atmosphere of the room changed, grew tense as Coransee entered. The Housemaster radiated power in the way of a man not only confident but arrogant. A man who meant for people to stand in awe of him. A man Teray disliked instantly. The Pattern told Teray that he and Coransee were temperamentally incompatible. They could be said to be far apart in the Pattern. The reason for the distance might have been great temperamental dissimilarity, or dangerous similarity—similar inclinations toward dishonesty or greed, for instance. Whatever it was, it separated Teray and Coransee definitely, thoroughly.

The four visitors stood up as the Housemaster entered. Coransee was a big man, tall, well-muscled, but without the heavy, stocky look of Joachim. Teray found himself staring at Coransee's long cold face with a feeling that disturbed him because it was gone before he could recognize it. It took him a moment to realize that Coransee was looking at him in the same way. But Coransee was slower to cover his reaction. Teray had time to wonder whether what he had seen in the Housemaster's eyes, and for an instant in his thoughts, was recognition. But whatever it was, it faded quickly into puzzlement. Then Coransee's shield snapped into place and Teray got nothing more. Reflexively, Teray shielded his own thoughts but behind his shield he continued to wonder.

Suddenly, as though in attack, Coransee drove his massive mental strength hard against Teray's shield. He meant to break through it. There was no doubt of that. He had apparently seen something in Teray's thoughts that caught his attention. He wanted another look. he did not get it; Teray's shield held firm. Before Teray could respond to the unprovoked attack, Joachim spoke up angrily.

"Coransee! My apprentice is a guest in your House. He's given you no offense. What's the matter with you?"

For a moment Coransee stared at him in cold anger, stared at him as though he was an unwelcome intruder breaking into a private conversation. "Nothing is the matter," he said finally. "Your apprentice is a very able young man. I think I may have seen him before—perhaps in one of my visits to the school."

Joachim gave Teray no time to deny this. "You may have," he said. "Although I can't see why that would be reason for you to attack him now." Joachim took a deep breath, calmed himself. "His name is Teray. This is his wife Iray, and my outsider Jer."

Coransee nodded, acknowledging all three introductions at once. But his attention had fastened on Teray.

"Teray," he repeated, drawing the word out thoughtfully. "How did you happen to choose a name ending in 'ray,' boy?"

The "boy" rankled, but Teray pretended to ignore it. "I'm told that I'm one of the sons of Patternmaster Rayal," he answered. His name had attracted attention before but he had fought for it and won the right to keep it while still in school.

"Rayal?" Coransee raised an eyebrow. "Rayal's children must number in the hundreds by now. But you're the first I've found who thought himself worthy to take his father's name."

Teray shrugged. "An adult is free to take any name. I chose to share my father's."

"And cause your wife to share it too, I see."

"No, Lord. She came to me freely and chose her own name."

"Did she." Coransee's attention seemed to wander. He had relaxed slightly, thinning his total shield down to a more comfortable heavy screen. For a moment, something flickered so close to the surface of his thoughts that Teray almost had it. He could have had it if he had dared to be obvious about his probing. But he let it pass. Abruptly, Coransee changed the subject.

"Joachim, I have an artist for you."

The sudden switch obviously surprised Joachim as much as it did Teray. But Joachim was cautiously enthusiastic. "An artist? I've been around the sector looking for a good one to work with some of my outsiders."

"I know." For the first time, Coransee smiled. "And this one is special. Sensitive. Fantastically sensitive."

Joachim began to draw in even his cautious enthusiasm.

17

"They're usually more than a little crazy when they're too sensitive. They don't have enough control of their ability to receive selectively."

"Oh, this boy has all the control he needs. Picks up latent images from anybody—Patternists, mutes, animals, even Clayarks. How many artists do you know who can lay their hands on a boulder that a Clayark has leaned against and read you the story of that Clayark's life?"

"Clayarks?"

"Test him."

"I've never had an artist who could pick up Clayark images. Call him."

Coransee turned toward the group of women and outsiders near the fireplace and called, "Laro!"

One of the outsiders in the group got up at once and came over to Coransee. He was a young man, probably only a few years older than Teray. Short and small-boned, he moved with quick, fluid grace. The Pattern betrayed him as a man of little mental strength. However competent he was at his art, he could never be anything more than an outsider. If he was lucky, his talent would buy him a comfortable place in someone else's House, and he would be troubled by none of the competitive spirit that sent stronger people out to found Houses of their own. If he was unlucky and did have such spirit, it would soon get him killed.

Coransee introduced the artist. "Laro, this is Lord Joachim and some members of his House. His people are artists and craftsmen."

Laro lowered his head and spoke respectfully. "My Lord." He was close to Joachim in the Pattern, Teray realized. That meant Joachim would probably buy him. Joachim's people were able to form themselves into the deadly fighting machine that Clayarks avoided only because Joachim chose them so carefully. He chose them not only for their skill and strength, but for their compatibility within the Pattern. The Pattern was a vast network of mental links that joined every Patternist with the Patternmaster. Its first purpose was supposed to be to give the Patternmaster the strength he needed—strength drawn through the links from the Patternists—to combat large-scale Clayark attacks. Actually, though, the Pattern was more often used as Joachim used it, as Teray was using it now. To judge, roughly, the mental strength of other Patternists, and to judge, more precisely, their compatibility.

Teray brought his attention back to the two Housemasters and realized that Coransee was listing the artist's accomplishments—doubtless to make the young man look as attractive as possible before they began talking about a price. Neither Housemaster was paying any attention to Teray, and Teray had no interest in the bargaining to come. He touched Iray lightly and started to go over to the group that Laro had left. Iray, evidently remembering Joachim's instructions, started to follow. Coransee stopped them.

"Teray, Iray, wait." He smiled again. He had an open, friendly smile that Teray would have trusted on anyone else. "View Laro's work with us." A command disguised as an invitation.

Caught, Teray and Iray came back slowly and sat down. Teray watched as the artist went past him and crossed the huge room to the group of women and outsiders that he had just left. From them he took three ceramic figurines and a small painting. Teray realized now why the group had seemed so absorbed. The artist had been entertaining them. Now Joachim's party was to sample his work.

Laro handed the painting to Joachim. The figurines went to Teray, Iray, and Jer. Teray first thought his was a wild animal. Not until he held it did he realize that the well-muscled four-legged body was human-headed. The thing was a Clayark.

Teray stared at it with interest. He had seen pictures of Clayarks at the school, but nothing as lifelike as this. His hands could almost feel warmth and a texture of flesh.

He folded his hands around the figurine, closed his eyes, and opened his mind to whatever experience awaited him. He expected a jolt. He had prepared himself for it—but not nearly enough.

Abruptly, shockingly, Teray was the Clayark. There was no time for anticipation, no disorientation. He felt himself seized and possessed by the artist-implanted "consciousness" of the figurine. Fortunately, by the time Teray recovered enough to struggle, he had also recovered enough to know that he should not struggle. He was still the Clayark.

He was within a torch-lit cave in the mountains far to the east of Redhill. He could see the rough gray-rock walls and the fire of the torches. He was a member of a munitions clan. His people made the rifles with which other Clayarks hunted food and fought Patternists. Now, though, his mind was not on gun-making. Now he had been challenged.

The sleek young female who stood apart from other onlookers, watching and holding her head so high—she was his. She was the daughter of his mother's brother, and long promised to him. Only he had a right to her. Not this other, this dog with his long jowly muzzle of a face. The other, the challenger, was big both with fat and with muscle. Years of handling heavy metal weights had given him great strength. And years of stuffing his belly like a pig had made him slow and clumsy. Savagely, the Clayark who was Teray lunged at him.

As the Clayark, Teray bit and punched with heavily calloused hands—or forefeet. He seized and tore and gouged, all the while leaping about with speed and agility that his opponent could not match. All his opponent's power was in his massive arms. Or forelegs. As long as the Clayark Teray could avoid those arms, he was safe.

Then the Clayark Teray stumbled, and almost fell over a loose rock as he dodged one of his opponent's clumsy swipes. His hand closed around the rock as he leaped away.

He wheeled and charged again. This time he reared back on hind legs, which were more catlike than human. As his opponent reared eagerly to meet him and finally lay hands on him, Teray smashed the rock against the side of the creature's head. Then he stood back in triumph and watched while his opponent died.

Teray opened his eyes and stared at the small figurine in his hands. He could see its beauty, its perfection, even more clearly now. What was it the Clayarks called themselves? Sphinxes. Creatures out of ancient mythology, lion-bodied, human-headed. The description was not really accurate. The Clayarks were furless and tailless, and they did possess hands. But they were much more sphinx-es—creatures who were at least partly human—than they were the animals Teray had always considered them.

And outsiders were not necessarily the inferior people Teray had considered them. The artist Laro had done something that Rayal himself could not have done. No Patternist could read the mind of a Clayark directly. The disease the Clayarks carried gave them at least that much protection from their Patternist enemies. And only the most sensitive artist could lift latent impressions of Cla-yarks from objects the Clayarks had touched. Laro not only lifted those impressions, he refined them, amplified them, and implanted them in his figurines and paintings. Teray caught the artist's attention and sent him silent ap-preciation. Laro smiled.

Jer and Iray had finished their experiences as Teray had. All three waited now as Joachim gazed silently at the painting. No sign of what he was experiencing appeared on his face, but they all could see that he was completely absorbed in the painting. Finally, Joachim's show was over and he looked up.

He put down the painting and turned to Coransee, his eagerness barely veiled. "What do you want for him?"

Moments later, in Coransee's office, Teray, Joachim, Laro, and Coransee himself were seated, waiting for Coransee to name his price. Joachim had tried to send Teray to entertain himself with more of Laro's work, but Coransee had insisted on his sitting in on the bargaining.

"He's an apprentice," the Housemaster had said. "He might as well start learning right now." Then, about the trade:

"Joachim, I had to trade with another sector to get Laro. He's a rare find, and I had intended to keep him. He's not close to me or many of my people in the Pattern, but that's not as important to me as it is to you. I'll trade him to you, though, if he agrees to the trade."

At once, Laro spoke up. "I do agree, Lord. I've been content here. I mean no disrespect. But Lord Joachim and his people seem much closer to me in the Pattern."

Coransee nodded. "That's what I thought. We trade then, Joachim."

Joachim leaned back in his chair. "As I asked before, what do you want for him?"

"I trade for strength, as always," Coransee said. "The success of the last Clayark raid makes it obvious that I don't have enough."

"If you were trading with anyone else, I'd advise you to trade for compatibility within the Pattern," said Joachim. "With more compatibility, you wouldn't have any of the Clayarks who attacked you still alive and dangerous. But you're trading with me and I don't have anyone even close to you in the Pattern."

"Would you be willing to trade Jer, the outsider you brought with you?" Coransee asked. Teray frowned. It seemed to him that the Housemaster was less serious than he should have been. Teray got the feeling that he had no interest at all in Jer.

"Jer's young," said Joachim, going along with him. "Only two years past transition. But he has the strength you're looking for."

"You would trade Jer?" asked Coransee softly.

"If you wanted him."

"I don't, of course."

"No."

"I just wondered. You're sentimental about your people sometimes. But you want this artist. I can see that. You'd trade anyone short of your lead wife for him."

Joachim looked uncomfortable. Coransee was playing with him. Dangling the artist temptingly before him, but refusing to name a price. And doing it all in a mildly insulting way.

"Coransee, for the third time, will you tell me what you're trading for?"

"Of course," said Coransee. "Of course. I offer you Laro for Teray."

The words were said so casually that it seemed to take Joachim a moment to digest them. More likely, though, Joachim used his moment of "surprised silence" to think of a negative answer that would not close the trading.

Teray looked from one man to the other. He had known what Coransee was going to say just an instant before he said it. Joachim had probably known too. Coransee had been a little too eager, had not concealed his thoughts as carefully as he might have. In his carelessness, he had permitted Teray to learn one other thing—a thing that was somehow part of the reason why the Housemaster wanted Teray badly enough to trade a talent like Laro's. A talent that had surely cost him several of his people.

But perhaps it would not matter. Already Joachim was turning down the offer.

"Coransee, I've told you this man is an apprentice, not an outsider. He's not my property. In fact, as an apprentice he's still under the protection of the school. I can't legally trade him."

"And you wouldn't if you could." Coransee spoke lazily, as though he had gotten the answer he expected and was merely playing another game. "Let's be realistic, Joachim. You want my artist, I need your apprentice. Laro is much closer to you in the Pattern than Teray is. And law or no law, Teray would have no power to object if you traded him."

Surprisingly, Joachim seemed to reconsider for a moment. Teray, watching him, felt the beginnings of fear. He had waited so long to avoid being taken as an outsider. If now, on his first day out of the school, all his waiting was to prove in vain . . .

"You were talking about strength," Joachim was saying. "Now that the Clayarks have found a way to get into the sector undetected, I'll be needing Teray's strength myself."

"For what? That miniature Pattern of yours would wipe out any Clayarks who haven't heard what a waste of time and lives it is to attack you."

"Even a miniature Pattern can always use additional strength."

"I protect the school," said Coransee. "I need the strongest outsiders I can get for the good of the school."

Joachim made a sound of disgust. "You don't even expect me to believe that. What is it really, Coransee? Why do you want my apprentice so badly?"

"Perhaps because he's another son of Patternmaster Rayal?" Teray spoke for the first time. "One of my many brothers?" His questions were not really questions but he looked toward Coransee as though expecting him to answer.

Coransee stared at him blankly for a moment. Then he smiled without humor and spoke to Joachim. "You see? Already he proves his usefulness to me. I was careless about maintaining my shield, and immediately he reminded me." And to Teray, "What else did you pick up . . . brother?"

By now Teray knew that he had made a mistake. He should have kept his findings—and the strength and stealth of his probe—to himself. But it was too late now. No lie would get past an alerted Coransee.

"Only your determination to make me your outsider, Lord."

"And how do you feel about that determination?"

Perhaps it was the condescending man-to-child tone of Coransee's voice that made Teray shut out the urgent warnings Joachim was sending and answer in his own way.

"Slavery has never appealed to me, Lord."

Something hardened in Coransee's voice. "You consider outsiders slaves then. And, of course, you would never voluntarily become a slave, would you?"

Teray! Joachim finally managed to make his thought felt. *Stay out of this! You don't know what you're doing. The more you antagonize him, the less chance we have.*

I won't become his outsider, Joachim. Teray screened heavily, protecting the thought from Coransee's interception.

You will if you don't stop talking and let me handle it. I've got the rest of the day to talk him out of it.

He won't be talked out of it. He's made up his mind. I'm going to have to face him sooner or later, no matter what.

If you're foolish enough to attack him, Teray, I'll help him against you myself. Now be quiet and fade into the background with Laro!

The intensity of Joachim's anger burned into Teray. He had no doubt that that Housemaster was completely serious. The dialogue had taken place in only a few seconds, so there had been no more of a pause in his conversation with Coransee than Coransee's last questions deserved. Now he still had to answer that question and do it in a way that would not lead to his deeper involvement. Somehow. He was about to speak when Joachim took the matter out of his hands.

"Are you trading with me, Coransee, or with my apprentice?" he asked angrily.

Coransee turned slowly to look at Joachim. Teray was startled at the relief he felt to have the man's eyes off him.

"Don't you think the boy should have something to say about this?" asked Coransee.

"You said it yourself." Joachim ran the words on both the vocal and mental level for emphasis. "What we decide, he will have to accept. He shouldn't even be here. Neither should the artist."

"All right," Coransee agreed. Teray wondered, under his renewed fear, how it felt to Joachim to have his most serious words answered with no more than mild amusement. "But the boy is right, you know. Sooner or later he will have to face me."

Teray said nothing, sent no parting thought as he left the office. Coransee's casual undetected eavesdropping into his conversation with Joachim was no more than payment for his own earlier snooping. But it angered him. No one should have been able to bypass his screens so easily without being noticed. He had been careless himself. It would not happen again.

He located Iray as quickly as he could, then managed to find a private corner where he could tell her what had happened.

She heard him, her eyes widening with disbelief as he spoke. Then before she could respond, a mute interrupted them with an offer of cool drinks and food . . . . It was the first time he could recall her being harsh with a mute.

"Get away from us! Leave us alone!" *Teray, what are you saying?*

"Speak aloud," he ordered. "And screen. This will be all over the house soon enough."

But Joachim wouldn't . . .

"Iray!"

She switched in mid-sentence. " . . . trade you. He wouldn't. He needs you. You're the strongest man he's ever been able to fit into his House."

"I didn't say he was going to trade me. I said Coransee wants him to."

"But why?"

"I don't know." Teray frowned. "He's found that he's my brother—half-brother, probably. It has something to do with that."

"What difference could that make?"

"I tell you, I don't know."

"It must be something else. Maybe he really does need your strength now that the Clayarks are raiding him."

"He can use my strength. But he doesn't really need it. He didn't even expect us to believe him when he said that."

"Maybe he just wants to do something to Joachim—get even with him for something." She shook her head angrily, bitterly. "Maybe he just likes being a son of a Clayark bitch!" She stood leaning against him, radiating her anger. "Joachim won't let it happen," she said. "He must have expected some kind of trouble, the way he kept warning us. But we can depend on him."

"I hope so. But there was something . . . at the last, when he made me leave, he threatened to help Coransee against me if I attacked."

"He was angry. He didn't mean it."

"He was angry, all right. But he meant it. He would have done it."

She opened her mouth to protest again, to defend Joachim. Then she closed it and lowered her head. "It can't happen, Teray." She seemed to surrender to the fear that she had been holding at bay with her anger. She pressed herself against him, trembling. "Don't you see what it would mean?" she whispered. "The outsider restrictions."

He said nothing, only looked at her. He knew which restriction she had in mind. There were several: outsiders were not free to father children as they wished, and of course they had little or no say in where they lived or how long they lived there. They were property. But the restriction Iray had in mind was the one that said outsiders could not marry. They were free enough to have all the sex they wanted with any woman in the House who would have them—as long as they were careful to father no unauthorized offspring. But if, as in Teray's case, a man was married before he lost his freedom, his wife took her place among the women of the House, the Housemaster's wives. And she became the only woman in the House permanently forbidden to her former husband.

The laws were old, made in harsher times. Perhaps it was reasonable, as the old records said, to forbid weak men to sire potentially weak children. But what reason could there be for denying a man access to his chosen one, his first, while permitting him so many others? What reason but to remind him constantly that he was a slave?

Teray drew a ragged breath. No matter why the laws had been made, they were still in effect, being used every day. Now, if Joachim failed him, they would be used against him.

No, he had chosen Joachim as well as been chosen by him. He knew the man. Iray was right. Joachim would not make the trade.

When they had talked for a while longer, Teray assuring Iray, reassuring himself, another mute approached them to say that Joachim had decided to stay the night. They had been assigned a room. If they wished to go there now . . .

They had dinner in their room that night, served by a young mute girl who knew enough to go about her work without bothering them. The girl was on her way out when, finally, Joachim came to see them. The mute girl smiled at him and continued out of the room. Joachim watched silently until she closed the door behind her.

Then he crossed the room to them, still silent. Teray stood up.

Joachim faced him, met his eyes. "I'm sorry, Teray."

"Sorry?" Teray repeated the word mechanically, then explosively: "Sorry! You mean you did it? You traded me?"

"Yes."

"Joachim, no!" Iray almost screamed the words. Then she was on her feet too, and beside Teray. "You've betrayed us." She radiated more anger than fear. "After I introduced you to Teray."

"How could you do it?" Teray demanded. "Why would you do it?"

Joachim turned away, went to stand beside a window. "You heard him. He wanted you. I couldn't stop him."

"Then why didn't you let me try?"

"You can try if you want to." Joachim shook his head wearily. "You probably will, sooner or later, because he wants you to. He wants to know just how strong you are. And he wants you to know his strength. He wants to put you in your place."

"You're so sure that I have no chance against him?"

"No chance at all. In a few years, maybe, when you've had more training, more experience, when you learn more control. But now . . . he'll humiliate you before the rest of his House, before Iray." He looked at Iray. "And that will be that."

"That's already that as far as you're concerned," said Iray.

Joachim said nothing.

"After all, you've sold us, and you've been paid." Her

voice was harder than Teray had ever heard it. "You're sorry! What do you want? Our forgiveness?"

Joachim answered softly, "I tried. I did everything I could to make him change his mind."

"I don't believe that. Either you wanted the artist and you did what was necessary to get him, or you let Coransee frighten you into making the trade." She looked at him closely. "You are afraid of him, aren't you?"

Startled, Teray looked at Joachim. The Housemaster looked tired, looked almost sick. But he did not look frightened.

"I'm afraid for Teray," said Joachim softly, "and for you."

"Then help us," demanded Teray. "We need your help, not your fear!"

"I can't help you."

"You mean you won't help us. No one outsider is worth the trouble you could give him for taking me. You wouldn't even have to fight."

"Teray, it doesn't have to be as bad as you think, being an outsider." There was desperation in Joachim's voice. "If you can just accept it, stop fighting Coransee, he can teach you more than I ever could. And he's not as far from you in the Pattern as you think."

"And what about me, My Lord?" If there had been any of Iray's childishness left, it was gone now. "Will it also be 'not as bad as I think' with my husband forbidden to me, and his slaver my owner!"

Joachim shook his head, his pain clear in his expression. He reached out to her, but she was closed to him. He took her by the shoulders and held her when she tried to turn away. "If I could help, do you think you would even have to ask me?"

Teray watched him silently for a moment, then, "Tell us why you can't help, Joachim." He thought he knew why. Joachim's anguish was real enough. But he still showed no signs of the fear that Iray had thought she had seen.

Joachim released Iray and turned to look at Teray. "You know, don't you?" he asked softly. "You're too good. You see too much. It got you into trouble this afternoon. Finished any hope I might have had of talking Coransee out of the trade. Too good."

"Tell us why you can't help," Teray repeated. He did know now, but he wanted to hear Joachim say it.

"I wonder how long it will take him to make an outsider of you," Joachim said.

Teray waited.

"All right!' Joachim seemed to have to force himself to go on. "I'm conditioned . . . controlled! That special horse of mine has more freedom than I have when it comes to dealing with Coransee."

Iray looked at him with disgust. "Controlled? Like a mute? Like an animal?"

"Iray!" Teray wondered why he bothered to stop her. Did Joachim still have pride to save? Did it matter? He was alone. Joachim was useless. What was he going to do?

"Do you know why I allowed him to plant his controls, Teray?"

Teray did not know. Or care. He said nothing.

"Because I wasn't as patient as you were. Because I left the school too soon. And I left alone except for my wife.

Coransee picked me up, forced me into his House as an outsider." Joachim hesitated. "So you see, I know what you're both going through. I had been with him seven years when he offered me a chance for freedom. I had to cooperate with him, let him plant his controls in my mind. It's delicate work—the planting. Not like just linking with someone. As strong as he is, even he couldn't have done it if I had resisted. So I didn't resist. By then, I would have done anything to get free. Anything."

"You call what you have now freedom?" Teray's own contempt was coming through.

"Yes!" said Joachim vehemently. "So will you after a few years of captivity." Then his tone changed, became what it had been earlier—saddened, hopeless. "No. I've been 'free' for years now and Coransee's controls have been in place every minute. He doesn't need my cooperation to hold them. I think I'll wear them for the rest of my life." He shrugged. "He doesn't use them often. But when he does, there's nothing I can do."

A contrite Joachim was no more helpful than an angry one. Teray wanted to ask him to leave. But then he would be alone with Iray, and she would ask him the questions that he was already asking himself. He had no answers even for himself. What could he do?

Joachim talked on, but he had changed his tone again. Now he spoke quietly with anger. "Teray, you were wise enough to stay under the protection of the school until you were accepted for apprenticeship. You were careful. You did everything right. Yet through my weakness and Coransee's dishonesty, you've lost your wife and your freedom. All while you were supposed to be under my protection. No matter what hold Coransee has on me, I can't just go away and forget about you."

"What will you do?" Teray asked resignedly. He already knew the answer.

"I can't do anything directly. You know that. But indirectly, I'll do everything I can, including an appeal to Rayal if necessary." Joachim was moving toward the door and Teray was relieved to see him going.

Parting words: "Teray, believe me, I'll get you away from him."

Teray did not believe him. Nor did he bother to pretend. He went to the door and opened it. "Good-bye, Joachim."

Joachim looked at him a moment longer as though trying to instill belief in his good intentions. As though he would have reached out to Teray if he had not feared finding Teray closed to him. Then he was gone.

Teray turned to Iray and saw that she was trembling.

"What are you going to do?" she whispered.

"I don't know." He ran a hand over his brow and was not surprised to have it come away wet. "I don't know. Maybe tomorrow . . ."

She was shaking her head. "Now, Teray. Don't you feel it? Coransee is coming now."

• Two •

As Iray spoke, both she and Teray received Coransee's wordless announcement of his presence, a mental image of the Housemaster standing outside Teray's door.

With mechanical politeness, Teray returned an image of Coransee inside the room. Not that he wanted Coransee inside. He was not ready for a confrontation. He had had no time to gather his thoughts, decide what battle strategy might give him the best chance. If he had a chance at all. Joachim had left him all but drained of confidence, of hope. Yet he had to fight.

But did he have to fight now?

As Coransee entered, Teray glanced back to Iray. She was watching him, her expression frightened, questioning, her eyes bright with unshed tears. Yes. He had to fight now. A duel, one to one, unless he wanted to give Coransee an excuse to call in members of his huge Household.

Coransee came into the room and stood near the door, looking from one of them to the other. He gave his head a weary half shake and sighed. "Now, eh, brother?"

Teray glared at him.

"Bad timing," continued Coransee. "You're tired and

emotionally drained. You should have chosen to wait. I would have let you spend the night here with Iray like a guest, and you could have fought me in the morning when you were rested."

He spoke as though humoring an irrational person—as though chiding a child. Hot with shame and anger, Teray struck.

He meant to kill as quickly as he could. He knew he had no chance against a man of Coransee's strength and experience unless he could get through Coransee's shielding and bludgeon him to death at once. Given time, Coransee could outmaneuver him, kill him with tricks instead of strength.

But Coransee's mental shielding seemed to absorb the blow without damage. Coransee slammed back with crushing force. Perhaps he too wished to end the fighting quickly. He struck again and again with almost-physical impact. Teray stumbled back against the bed, his shield withstanding the assault but his senses reeling. Blows were openings, were pathways to be traced back to their source. No Patternist could strike a blow through his own solid shield. To strike was to open one's own shield, however slightly, however briefly, and make oneself vulnerable. it was part of Teray's strength that he could strike with mind-blurring speed through a pinhole of an opening. It was part of Coransee's strength and experience that he could strike Teray repeatedly without Teray being able to get a fix on one of his blows and trace it back before Coransee's shield became solid again.

Teray knew at once that he had met his match.

Coransee was at least as fast and as strong as he was. At least.

He hammered at Teray's shield with a ferocity that left Teray able to do nothing more than maintain that shield and endure.

Still, it was a standoff. Teray was enduring and Coransee was probably wearing himself out. Teray waited, shaken, jolted, but not really hurt—waited for his chance.

But because Coransee was hammering at Teray's shield so continuously, Teray was only half aware of what was happening to his body. He realized that someone had grasped his wrist but it took him longer to realize that the someone was Coransee.

Contact! Coransee was so occupied with keeping Teray subdued that he wanted physical contact to help him focus a second kind of attack, and do physical harm. The realization came too late. It came after Teray realized that something had happened to his heart.

Teray found himself clutching his chest in pain. He was suddenly not breathing properly, gasping, coughing. The pain seemed to spread and worsen. Teray tore his wrist away from Coransee, but the Housemaster had already done his work. The pain continued, grew. He could have stopped it, but if he gave his attention to his body, Coransee would be free to break down the defenses of his mind.

But his heart. He was dying.

Somehow, he began again to strike at Coransee, to throw all his strength into a new attack. If he lived, he could repair his body later. If he died, he meant to take his brother with him.

Suddenly Coransee ceased his own battering attack, and withdrew behind a total shield. Perhaps he was tiring. Desperately, Teray hit harder. But his body hampered him. He was slowing, faltering.

Teray became aware of Coransee tracing a blow back through Teray's shield. And even aware of him, Teray was too slow to shut him out.

Coransee had his foothold. He slashed at the rest of Teray's shielding, his mind a machete. Teray felt his shielding being stripped away. He tried to hold it, struggling to remain conscious. Coransee grasped him, held him, blasted him into oblivion.

To Teray's utter surprise, he regained consciousness on the bed of the guest room, with Iray looking down at him. He had not expected to regain consciousness at all.

He moaned and closed his eyes again. He felt weak but he was in no pain. Apparently, Coransee or Iray had already made whatever repairs his body needed. He felt hungry the way people did after being healed, but it was a bearable hunger. He had only recently eaten part of his dinner. Iray had been sitting up. Now she lay down beside him. He put his arm around her and drew her closer so that her head rested on his shoulder. How to say it? How to tell her he was sorry?

"Iray . . ."

She put a hand over his mouth. "Didn't I see? Don't you think I know what you feel?"

He shook his head silently, his body suddenly trembling with shame and fury. He made a ragged sound of anguish and twisted away from her. He wanted to go down and take Coransee on again—make him finish the job this time. He wanted to kill, or to die. He had lost everything. Everything! Why hadn't Coransee killed him?

Iray tried to turn his head, make him face her. He caught hold of her hands and looked at her. He had lost her. What was she even doing there?

"I'll get us out of this," he said. "I swear . . ."

"Teray . . ."

"I won't stop trying until—"

"Teray, listen! There's a way out."

He broke off, staring at her. "What?"

"Listen. Coransee said you were to report to him tomorrow . . . tomorrow morning. He said he might make you his apprentice. You're stronger than he thought. He said you'd make a better ally than servant. Teray, he said I might . . . we might be able to stay together."

"Might?"

"He wants to talk to you. I don't know why. And he said he had to find out something from the school. But we have a chance, Teray. At least a chance."

"Maybe. But what is there to talk about—or find out? Either I'm an apprentice or I'm not."

"You could learn more from him than from Joachim. Much more. And maybe you'd be able to have your own House sooner."

Teray shook his head wearily. "Love, don't put so much of your trust in him. I don't know what he has in mind, but . . ."

"Teray, whatever it is, go along with him." She was leaning over him, looking down into his eyes. "Please. Go along with him. I don't want to be a *thing* won in a fight. I want to be your wife. Please."

He drew a ragged breath. "Do you think I'd miss a chance—any real chance—to get what we both want?"

She seemed to relax. She kissed him and brought him to stronger awareness of her body softly against him. She was what he needed now. He slipped his arms around her. She would always be what he needed.

Early the next morning, as the rest of the House awoke and began the day's work. Teray announced himself outside Coransee's private quarters. He stood in the great common room that he had entered the day before with Joachim. He had not realized then how big the room was. The fireplace seemed a long way off at the other end of the room. Right now there were two mutes in it, cleaning it. There were couches, chairs, and low tables scattered around the room, and the walls were lined with cases of books, learning stones, game boards, small figurines, and more. Yet the room was not cluttered. In fact, at this hour, it seemed far too empty. There were only a few mutes cleaning, and a Patternist who had chosen for some reason to come down the front stairs and walk around to the huge dining room.

Abruptly, Teray received Coransee's invitation to enter. Teray followed the invitation and found himself not in the Housemaster's office but in a comfortable-looking carpeted sitting room. There, Coransee, wearing only a black robe of some glossy material, was having breakfast, served to him by a blond mute woman. The woman had set two places.

Coransee glanced at Teray and waved him into the empty chair at the small window table. Just as though they hadn't been trying to kill each other only hours before, Teray thought. He sat down, was served steak and eggs from the mute's cart, and, like Coransee, ate silently until the mute left. Then Coransee spoke.

"Have you ever seen our father, Teray?" His tone was surprisingly friendly.

"No."

"I thought not. You look like him, though—much more than I do. That's what caught my attention about you yesterday."

Teray was interested in spite of himself. Rayal did almost no traveling. Probably only a small fraction of the Patternists had actually seen him. He was the Pattern. He was strength, unity, power. Every adult Patternist was linked to him, but the link did not involve tracing out his features. Most Patternists neither knew nor cared what he looked like.

"You and I are full brothers, you know," said Coransee. Same father *and* mother. I awakened the Schoolmistress last night to find that out, though I already suspected it."

Teray shrugged. He knew nothing of his mother. Rayal had many wives.

"Our mother was Jansee, Rayal's sister and lead wife."

Teray froze, a forkful of steak halfway to his mouth. He put down the fork and looked at Coransee. "So that's it."

"That's it."

"Are you going to kill me?"

"If I was, you would have died last night."

Teray turned his attention back to his food, not wanting

to be reminded of his defeat. The informality of the scene suddenly seemed incongruous to him. He had expected to stand before Coransee's desk like an errant schoolboy and listen to the Housemaster's sarcasm. Yet here he was having breakfast with Coransee. And not once had he called the Housemaster "Lord." Nor would he, Teray decided. He might as well find out now just how far he could go. What could Coransee possibly want?

"As it is," said Coransee, "we both might live. It would be best if we did, now that our father is dying."

"Dying? Now?"

"He's been cheating death for twenty years," said Coransee. "Even at the school, you must have learned that."

"That he has the Clayark disease, yes. But I thought you meant he was really about to die from it."

"He is."

Teray ate silently, refusing to ask more questions.

"He's let me know that he can last perhaps a year longer," said Coransee. He lowered his voice slightly. "Do you want the Pattern, brother?"

"You're asking me if I want you to kill me."

"I mean to succeed Rayal."

"I can see that."

"So you're right. If you contest, I will have to kill you."

"Others will contest. You won't just step into Rayal's place."

"I'll worry about them when they reveal themselves. Now, you are my only concern."

Teray said nothing for a long moment. He had never really thought that he had a chance to succeed Rayal. The

Patternmaster simply had too many children, a number of them not only older but, like Coransee, already Masters of their own Houses. Clearly, though, Coransee thought Teray had a chance—and was now demanding that he give up that chance. Teray had no doubt that Coransee could and would kill him if he refused. If the Housemaster was not actually stronger—and that was still in doubt—he was more versatile, more experienced. And if it was possible for Teray to live the kind of life he had planned for himself without fighting, he would rather not challenge his brother again.

"I won't contest," he said quietly. The words were surprisingly difficult to say. To be Master of the Pattern, to hold such power . . .

"I let you live thinking that you wouldn't." Coransee looked across at him calculatingly. "Shall I accept you as my apprentice?"

Teray tried to conceal his sudden excitement. He met Coransee's eyes with simulated calm. Was it going to be this easy? "I would willingly become your apprentice."

Coransee nodded. "What I'm trying to do," he said, "is use you to avoid making the mistake our father made."

"Mistake?"

"When our mother allied herself with him, he let her live. He wanted someone as powerful, or nearly as powerful, as he was to be ready to take the Pattern if anything happened to him. Someone he could trust not to try to snatch it away from him ahead of time. But he kept Jansee with him. Made her his wife instead of permitting her to set up a House of her own in some other sector. That meant that when trouble came to him, she was vulnerable to it too. And as it happened, it killed her instead of leaving her to take over for him.

"Now, to prevent that from happening again, I want to leave you here at Redhill. When the time comes, I'll have to move to Forsyth, to the House of the Patternmaster."

Teray frowned, not daring to understand what Coransee seemed to be saying. "Brother . . . ?"

"You've understood me, I see. When the Pattern is mine, this House will be yours. I'll take from it only the closest of my wives, and a few outsiders. The rest I will leave to you."

Teray shook his head, fearing to believe. It was too much, and far too easy. "You offer me all this at no cost? You give it to me?"

"What price could you pay me?"

"None. You're right. I have nothing."

"Then you have nothing to lose." He paused. "I do ask something. But it's not what you would call a price."

Teray looked at him with sudden suspicion, but Coransee went on without seeming to notice.

"It's more like a guarantee. Brother, I have to know that when you're older and more experienced you won't decide that you gave up the Pattern too easily. I have to be certain that you'll be content as a Housemaster and not decide to try for Patternmaster."

"I've said it," said Teray. "I'll open to you, let you see for yourself that I mean it."

"I already know you mean it. I know you aren't lying to me. But a man can change. What you believe now might not be worth anything five or ten years from now."

"But you'd hold the Pattern by then. You could stop me from any attempt to usurp . . ."

"Perhaps I could—and perhaps not. But I'm not about to wait and find out the hard way."

Teray knew the price now. He found himself thinking of Joachim. Controlled. But he recalled Joachim's words. Coransee needed the cooperation of his victim if he was to plant his controls. he could not do it unless Teray let him.

"I want you alive for the sake of the people," said Coransee. "We've got Clayarks chewing at the borders of every sector from the desert to the northern islands. They know Rayal has been too much concerned with keeping himself alive to give proper attention to raiders. When he finally gives up the power and dies, I mean for the people to have security again. But I won't permit you to be a threat to my security."

"I'm not a threat," said Teray stubbornly.

"You know what assurance I want, brother. Your words aren't worth anything to me."

"You're asking me to step from physical slavery into mental slavery!"

"I'm offering you everything you claim to want. Are you getting ambitious already? My controls would do nothing other than make certain you kept your word."

"Joachim told me how you use your controls."

"Joachim!" Coransee did not bother to hide his contempt. "Believe me, brother, Joachim needs the controls I keep on him. Without them, he would never have succeeded in taking a House of his own."

"How could he, as your outsider?"

"He became my outsider through his own bad judgment. Just as he accepted you for apprenticeship through bad judgment."

"You mean because he wasn't as suspicious of me as you are? Because he believed me when I let him see that I wasn't after his House?"

"Teray, the moment he realized that you are stronger than he is—you are, by the way, and he knew it—he should have dropped you. That's common sense. When you're Master of your own House, see how you feel about accepting an underling who just might learn enough from you to snatch your House away."

"Did you help Joachim win his House from its previous Master?"

"Indirectly. I gave him some special training."

"But why? And why keep control of him?"

Coransee gave him a long, calculating look. "Sector politics," he said finally. "I wanted to be certain of a majority vote on the Redhill Council of Masters. Joachim's predecessor opposed me very loudly, very stupidly."

The warning was unmistakable. Teray sighed. "I don't oppose you," he said. "How can I? But I can't pay your price either. I can't bargain away my mental freedom, sentence myself to a lifetime of mental slavery."

"How free do you think you are now?"

"Free at least to think what I want to."

"I see. Well, since you put so much stock in promises, I'd be willing to give you my word that I won't interfere with your thinking except to stop you from usurping power."

Teray glared at him.

After a moment, Coransee laughed aloud. "I see you're less naïve than you pretend to be. Thank heavens for that. But listen, brother, noble lies aside, just how much control over you do you think I want? You'd live your everyday life as free mentally as you are now. Why not? I haven't the time nor the inclination to meddle into the petty details of someone else's life. The only thing you won't be free to do is oppose me. All my controls would do is put you at the same level as everyone else, once I'm Pattern-master. You'll be different only in that your strength makes it necessary for me to have an extra hold on you—a hold beyond the Pattern. You have no more reason to object to my controls than you have to object to your link with the Pattern."

"The Pattern is different. It doesn't control anyone's thinking." Teray drew a deep breath and said bluntly, "Even if I thought I could trust you—even if you were Joachim, whom I did trust—I couldn't accept the leash, the brand that you want to put on me."

"Not even to save your life?" Coransee's voice remained quiet, conversational.

Teray opened his mouth to give him a defiant "No!" but somehow it was not that easy to say the word that could condemn him. He closed his mouth and stared down at his plate. Finally he found his voice. "I can't." The two words were so shamefully much weaker than the one would have been that he felt compelled to say more, to redeem himself. "What's the point of buying my life with the one thing I still have that makes it worth living? Go ahead and kill me."

Coransee leaned back and shook his head. "I wish I had

read you less correctly, brother. I thought that was what you would say. I will give you as much time as our father has left to change your mind."

Again Teray betrayed himself. He wanted to insist, as he believed, that he would never change his mind. But that would be like asking to be struck down now. He said nothing.

"I can only accept you as an apprentice on my terms," said Coransee. "Until you accept those terms, you remain an outsider, subject to all the outsider restrictions and observing all the formalities." He paused. "You understand."

"I . . . yes, Lord." As long as he was still alive, he had a chance. Or did he think that only because he wanted so badly to live? No, there was a chance. One could escape physical slavery. The physical leash was not as far-reaching or as permanent as the mental leash.

"As for your work," Coransee said, "one of my muteherds is due a promotion. He's in charge of the mutes who maintain the House and grounds. You will replace him."

"A muteherd?" Teray could not keep his dismay out of his voice. Caring for mutes was not only the job of an outsider, but, for the sake of the mutes, a weak outsider.

"That's right," said Coransee. "And you start today. Jackman, the man you're replacing, is waiting for you now."

"But, Lord, mutes . . ."

"Mutes! Damage them with your strength, and when you recover from the beating I'll surely give you, you'll find yourself herding cattle."

Jackman waited just outside the door to Coransee's private quarters. He was a tall, bony man with straw-colored

hair and mental strength so slight that he could easily
have been a teacher at the school. Teachers, even more
than muteherds, dealt with mentally defenseless people,
and were required to be relatively harmless themselves.
Jackman was harmless enough. He could not quite hide
his shock when he met Teray and, through the Pattern,
recognized Teray's greater strength.

"Son of a bitch," he muttered. "If you're not even-tem-
pered, you're going to kill every mute in the House."

At that moment Teray was feeling far less than even-
tempered, but he realized that Jackman was right. He
pushed aside his anger at Coransee and followed Jackman
up to the fourth-floor mute quarters, where his new room
would be.

A pair of mutes were already moving Jackman's things
out. One of them, the woman, was weeping silently as she
worked. Teray looked at her, then looked at Jackman.

"I'm taking her with me, if you don't mind," Jackman
said.

"Your business," said Teray.

"And yours." There was a note of disapproval in Jackman's voice. "Every mute in the House is your business
now."

It was not a responsibility Teray wanted to think about.
"You care about the mutes, don't you?" he asked Jackman. "I mean really care. It wasn't just a job to you."

"I care. Right now I'm downright worried about them.
I'm afraid you're going to wind up killing some of them
out of sheer ignorance before you find out how to handle
them."

"Frankly, so am I." Teray was getting an idea.

Jackman frowned. "Look, they're people, man. Powerless and without mental voices, but still people. So for God's sake try to be careful. To me, killing one of them is worse than killing one of us, because they can't do a damn thing to defend themselves."

"Will you show me what you know about them—how you handled them?"

Jackman's expression became suspicious. "I'll teach you what I can, sure."

"That isn't what I meant."

"I didn't think it was. What the hell gives you the idea you're entitled to anything more?"

"I'm not entitled. I just thought you might be willing to do the one thing you could do to safeguard your mutes."

"*Your* mutes! My mental privacy doesn't have a goddamn thing to do with it. Nobody but Coransee can make me do what you're asking."

"And I wouldn't ask it if other people's lives weren't involved. But I honestly don't want to kill any of these mutes. And without your help, I will."

"You're asking for my memories," said Jackman. "And you know as well as I do that you're going to wind up with a lot more than just my memories of muteherding."

"There's no other method of teaching that's fast enough to keep me from doing some damage."

"Nosing into my life isn't teaching."

Teray sat on the edge of the bed and stared at the floor. He had thought it would be easy, that a man so clearly attached to the mutes would be willing to sacrifice a little of his mental privacy for their good. He glanced at the two mutes still in the room. "You two leave us alone for a few minutes."

Irritatingly, the mutes looked at Jackman and received his nod before they obeyed.

"Don't hold it against them," Jackman said when they were gone. "They've looked to me for orders for five years. It's habit."

"Jackman, open to me voluntarily. I don't want to have to force you."

"You've got no right!" He tried to reach out to alert Coransee, but to do that he had to open his already-inadequate shield. Instantly, Teray was through the shield. He held Jackman trapped, isolated from contact with the rest of the House. He had the foolish urge to apologize to Jackman for what he was doing as he tapped and absorbed the man's memories of the previous five years. He wasn't doing to Jackman quite what Coransee wanted to do to him, but he was invading Jackman's mental privacy. He was throwing his weight around, acting like a lesser version of the Housemaster. And he wasn't even doing it solely for the good of the mutes. They were important, of course, but Teray was also avoiding a promised beating and a cattleherding assignment. Things were bad enough.

When Teray let Jackman go, he knew everything the older man did about keeping mutes. He also knew Jackman with great thoroughness. For instance, he knew what the muteherd was afraid of, knew what he could do to help him, and, perhaps to some degree, make up for invading his privacy.

"Jackman," he said, "I'm Coransee's brother—full brother. I might be second to him in strength here, but I don't think I'm second to anyone else. Now I know you're worried about having a rough time when you move to the third floor, and you're right to be. You're almost as weak as one of your mutes, and you're going to be everyone's pawn. If you want to, you can keep a link with me. After a couple of people try me out, no one will bother either of us."

"After what you just did, you think I'd hide behind you?"

Teray said nothing. He knew the man well enough now to realize that he had already said enough.

"You're trying to bribe me to keep my mouth shut about what you did," said Jackman. "Coransee'd make you think you were being skinned alive if I went to him."

This was a bluff. Teray knew from Jackman's own mind that Coransee generally let his outsiders find their own level within his House. He was not especially concerned about the strong bullying the weak, as long as the weak were not left with serious injuries—and as long as both strong and weak obeyed him when he spoke. Teray watched Jackman calmly.

Jackman glared back at him, livid with rage. Then, slowly, the rage dissolved into weary submission. "If there was any way for me to kill you, boy, I'd do it gladly. And slowly."

"I've linked us," said Teray. "If you get into trouble, I'll know. If I find that you caused the trouble to make trouble for me, I'll let you be torn apart. But if you didn't cause it, and you want my help, I'll help you. Nothing else. The link isn't a control or a snoop. Just an alarm."

"Like the kind some Patternist mothers keep on their kids to be sure the kids are okay, right?"

Teray winced. He would never have said such a thing. Why did Jackman go out of his way to humiliate himself?

"May as well call a thing what it is," said Jackman.

"The minute you decide you don't want the link, you can dissolve it. Right now if you like." Teray kept his attention on the link, making certain that Jackman was aware of it and that he saw that it was under his control, that he could indeed destroy it.

But Jackman made no move to destroy the link. He gave Teray an unreadable look. "You're not really doing this to bribe me to be quiet, are you?"

"It doesn't matter," said Teray.

Jackman grinned unpleasantly. "You're doing it to soothe your conscience, aren't you? Doing it to blot out the 'bad thing' you did before. You never really left the goddamn school, did you, kid?"

Teray struck Jackman in the carefully restrained way he had just learned to strike a mute. He hit Jackman a little harder than he would have hit a mute, because the mute-herd did have some defenses to get through. But on a physical parallel it was too much like slapping a child.

Jackman reeled back against the wall as though he had been hit physically. For a moment he stood still, bent slightly from the waist, his head down, cursing.

Teray reached out to find the two mutes. He located them easily, knowing their minds from Jackman's memories. With careful gentleness, he called them back into the room to finish moving Jackman's things. He used exactly the same amount of power that Jackman would have used.

The most important thing he had gotten from Jackman was a thorough knowledge of how much mental force mutes could tolerate without harm.

Jackman straightened the moment the two mutes came in. They looked at him curiously, then gathered up armloads of clothing and other possessions.

Jackman spoke to Teray once more as he and the mutes were leaving the room. "Conscience or not," he said quietly, "you're his brother all right." And strangely, it seemed that he said it with admiration.

• Three •

Teray searched for Iray using only his eyes. Had he used his mind, he could have found her in a moment. But he was not in that much of a hurry. He searched for her not knowing what he would say to her when he found her. Was it only the night before that he had promised her he would accept any chance he could get for freedom?

The thought reminded him painfully of Joachim.

He stopped, suddenly recalling Joachim's intention to spend the night at Coransee's house. Had he done it? Was he still there?

Teray reached out, swept his perception through the House, and found Joachim as quickly and easily as he could have found Iray. The Housemaster had a guest room in Coransee's quarters. And now that Teray had found him, he wondered whether he really wanted to see him. Why should he want to see him? Did he need advice from Joachim? Hadn't Joachim already told him that in a few years he too would view Coransee's mental controls as a small price to pay for freedom? For limited freedom. For the illusion of freedom.

But Teray was to have only one year, or less, to make that decision—if he made it at all."

Breaking away from his thoughts angrily, Teray reached out again and located Iray. She was in the courtyard, a large garden area three-quarters surrounded by the walls of the House.

He went to her and found her sitting alone on one of the concrete benches placed at intervals around the rectangular pathway. Teray stood still for a moment, looking around the garden. There was a fountain at its center, pleasantly breaking the morning quiet with the sound of falling water.

There were paths leading to the fountain and flowers between the paths. Outside the rectangle of the main path there were shrubs, some of them flowering, and trees. All this, Teray realized, was tended by his mutes. Thank heaven they already knew their work. Teray knew almost nothing about gardening—nor had Jackman known, Teray realized, examining the memories he had taken from the man. Jackman had never bothered to learn. He had simply let the mutes go on tending the garden as they had before he took charge of them.

Teray realized that he was still putting off speaking to Iray.

He went over and sat down beside her, felt her expectant waiting.

"I've failed you," he said quietly. "Again. I couldn't pay the price Coransee asked."

She was abruptly closed to him, shut behind a full shield, alone with herself. Physically, her reaction was mild. She sighed, and looked down at the hard-packed sandy reddish soil of the pathway. "Tell me what happened. Tell me all of it."

He told her. She had a right to know. And knowing, she had a right to hate him. He had sacrificed her freedom as well as his own. As he had trusted Joachim, she had trusted him. She was beautiful and strong in her own right. Not strong enough to establish a House of her own, but strong enough to make a secure place for herself in any existing House she chose. Other men had wanted her—established Housemasters. She had turned them down to stay with Teray. And now . . .

Teray finished his story, and drew a deep breath.

She turned and looked at him—looked at him for a long time. He grew uncomfortable under her gaze but he could think of nothing more to say.

"Are you going to let him kill you?"

Her words seemed to bring him to life. "Of course not! I wouldn't *let* anyone kill me!"

"What are you going to do?"

"Fight . . . again. If it comes to that. I'm not going to waste the time he's given me. I'm going to learn whatever I can. Maybe learn enough to . . ." He could not finish the sentence, the lie. No outsider would be watched more closely than he. No one would be more shielded from knowledge that might help him win his freedom. Yet he could not accept the final defeat. He could not do what Joachim had done.

Iray laid a hand on his shoulder, then raised it to his face. "I'm not going to change my name," she said.

He set his teeth, not wanting to say what he knew he

had to say. "You're going to do whatever is necessary. You have to make a place for yourself here."

"Teray . . ."

"I can't protect you. You . . . aren't my wife anymore. Perhaps you will be again. I'll fight for that. If I break free, I won't leave you here. But for now . . . we both know what you have to do."

"I'd like to help you kill him!"

"You know better. You hate him for what he's done to me! You can't afford to do that. Think of yourself. You're beautiful, and strong enough to rise high in any House. Please him, Iray. Please him!"

She sat silent, staring at the ground. After a while she got up and went back into the House.

The House mutes knew their jobs. They were well programmed and hardly needed Teray to direct them. For days he simply moved among them, permitting them to get used to him. It annoyed him to realize that they missed Jackman. They did not dislike Teray. Their programming did not permit them to dislike any Patternist. They simply preferred Jackman, whom they knew—and who had treated them kindly. Teray did not treat them in any way at all.

He could not focus his thoughts on them, could not really make himself care about them. His own problems held his attention, weighed on him. And it did not help him to see Coransee and Iray together around the House. Coransee had moved quickly. Sometimes in the morning Teray would see them coming out of Coransee's quarters together and going out on some business of Coransee's.

Several of Coransee's wives had begun to look at Iray with open jealousy. Clearly, she was becoming one of Coransee's favorites. And how did she feel about that?

She seemed subdued at first. Quiet, withdrawn, resisting emotionally what she could not resist physically. She was no actress. She had never been able to hide her feelings from Teray. Even when she closed her mind to him, her face and her mannerisms betrayed her. Teray watched her, concerned that she would anger Coransee with her stubbornness; though Teray took secret pride in that stubbornness. Then Iray began to smile, and Teray watched her with another kind of concern. Was she finally learning to act, or was her stubbornness beginning to melt?

Coransee was a handsome, powerful man. He could be charming. Several of his wives made no secret of the fact that they were in love with him. And Iray was young—just out of school. It was one thing for her to resist the attentions of wealthy lords who came to the school, where they could flaunt little of their wealth or power before her. Where they were just other men. But here on Coransee's vast estate . . . How much difference did it make?

Teray watched, sickened by the way Iray was beginning to look at Coransee. And Iray would no longer meet Teray's eyes at all.

And time was passing. And Teray was learning nothing, as he had feared. And Joachim, who had submitted, was at his home with his outsiders and wives and mutes—with the wealth and power that he controlled at least when Coransee left him alone.

Teray was solitary and morose. His mutes feared him. They knew, as he did, that it would be nothing new for an angry Patternist to take out his frustrations on the nearest mute. Of course, abusing mutes was illegal, was punished painfully when it was discovered. But the muteherd, guardian as well as supervisor of the mutes, could make certain that his violence went undiscovered. Years before, Rayal had swept the sectors regularly, seeking out and punishing instances of mute abuse and other lawbreaking. But there had been no such sweeps for some time. Rayal did nothing now except keep himself alive and in power. Thus, the mutes of Coransee's House watched Teray warily and leaped to obey when he spoke. It would never have occurred to him to abuse a person as helpless as a mute. Yet he could not summon the initiative to reassure them, ease their fear. He could not make himself really care. Not until the morning a frightened mute awoke him before dawn to tell that there had been an accident in the kitchen.

Teray got up silently, radiating annoyance that the mute could not feel, and followed the mute down to the huge kitchen. A cook had dropped a pan of hot cooking grease on his foot. The foot was badly burned.

Teray bent at once to examine the foot. He could read the man's pain on his face but he was careful not to read it in his mind. Like all Patternists, Teray had been taught as much as he could learn of healing before he left the school. The healing ability had little to do with mental strength. it was a different sort of power. Most Houses kept at least one woman or outsider who specialized in healing. One who could do massive work like regenerating limbs or ridding a body of some poison or deadly disease. A good healer could handle anything short of the

Clayark disease. But Teray was not a good healer. Carefully, he doused the man's agony. That was simple enough, but the healing . . .

He considered calling Coransee to find out who the healer of the House was. He should have found out long ago, he knew. And he knew that Coransee would tell him as much in no uncertain language. Then he remembered the large, only partially digested lump of his Jackman memories. He reached into them, and found the healer's name and the emergency mental call that she responded to. Knowing eased his mind, gave him confidence. If the healer was there and ready to answer quickly, then he could risk not bothering her. He could risk healing the mute himself.

He found it easiest to act as though the mute's body were his own, as though Teray were regenerating his own flesh. Much cooked, dead flesh had to be sloughed off. The mute's pain could not be allowed to return. Teray closed his eyes in concentration. He did not open them until he was finished. The mute's foot was whole again, and he sat gazing, fascinated, at the new pink flesh.

"It will be tender for a while," Teray told him. "But it's all right. Have a good breakfast and take the day off."

The mute smiled. "Thank you."

And Teray went back to bed feeling pleased with himself for the first time since he had become a muteherd. He had performed the healing slowly but properly. He would have had the House healer check the mute, but he felt certain that the man was completely well. Teray had not done such a thing for anyone other than himself since he had learned how to do it, years before.

Slowly he began to take an interest in the mutes. He had made no friends among the outsiders or the women of the House. And he had taken no woman to replace Iray, though he had noticed a few of the women looking at him with interest. A couple of them had even spoken to him, openly offering, but he had turned them down as gently as he could. It might be easier if he did not see Iray around the House nearly every day. It might be easier if he had more to do. His mutes still seemed too efficient. Except for an occasional healing, they did not need him. Or so he thought until a small red-haired mute woman named Suliana collapsed at his door one night.

Teray turned his attention from the history stone that he had been absorbing to the noise outside his door. Instantly he was overwhelmed by a wave of agony.

He gave a choked cry, screened himself from the pain, and hurried to the door. Suliana lay on the floor, half propped up by the door. Teray opened his mind a little more, still screening out the woman's pain. He became aware of the exact position of her body, then he opened the door carefully, catching her so that she would not fall and hit her head on the floor. She whimpered at his touch and he realized that most of her body was cut and bruised. And she had internal injuries. He lifted her gently, centering his total awareness on her body. She had two broken ribs, and if he handled her carelessly one of them would puncture her left lung. He put her on his bed and took away her pain. Then, knowing that he was out of his depth, he called the healer.

The healer's name was Amber. She was a golden-brown woman with hair that was a round cap of small, tight black curls. And she had a temper.

She took one look at Suliana lying silent on Teray's bed and attacked Teray.

"What the hell is wrong with you, letting this sort of thing go on! I thought you were a little better than Jackman—or at least stronger. I thought I'd repaired this poor girl for the last time when you took over."

"Hold on," said Teray, stepping away from her in surprise. "I don't know what you're talking about. Why don't you take care of Suliana, then tell me?"

"You don't know!" It was an accusation.

"No, I don't. Now let's wait until you've finished before we argue about whether or not I should. Take care of the mute."

She glared at him, radiating resentment, and he found himself recalling what he had learned at school—that even Housemasters were careful how they antagonized healers. A good healer was also a terrifyingly efficient killer. A good healer could destroy the vital parts of a person's body quickly enough and thoroughly enough to kill even a strong Patternist before he could repair himself. But Teray stood his ground. He had already angered her, apparently. He was not going to back down out of fear of her.

After a moment she turned from him with a sound of disgust and began working on Suliana. She gave the mute woman sleep, then silently worked over her for nearly an hour. Meanwhile, Teray reached down to the kitchen and ordered a large meal for Suliana. The healed usually needed food as soon as possible after their healing, since healers drew on the energy and nutrients of their patients' bodies to heal them. The food came as Amber was finishing, and the mute who brought it looked at Suliana sadly and murmured, "Again?"

As he left the room, Teray delved into his thoughts. It was time he found out what everyone else apparently already knew.

Suliana, he learned, was kept as the private property of an outsider named Jason. Two years before, Coransee had forced Jason into his House when Jason left the school with his wife. Later, Coransee had traded the wife to another House. Unfortunately for Suliana, she looked very much like Jason's wife. Thus, he had taken possession of her. Even more unfortunately for Suliana, she was not Jason's wife. Thus, periodically, in perverted anger and frustration, Jason beat the mute woman almost to death.

"Did you get it all?" asked Amber.

Teray realized that she had finished and was looking at him. "I got what that kitchen mute knew, anyway."

"And you didn't know anything about it?"

"Not consciously. I see now that I have knowledge of it from Jackman, though. And I see that it's been going on because Jackman was too frightened of Jason to go to Coransee about it."

"Your name is Teray, isn't it?"

"Yes."

"Teray, what the goddamn hell have you been doing for the past few weeks?"

Somehow, Teray held on to his temper. "You've made your point," he said quietly. "Now drop it."

"Why?" Her voice was dryly mocking. "Are you

ashamed? Good. If you can feel ashamed, I guess there's some hope for you. What are you going to do?"

He took a deep breath. No doubt he deserved her sarcasm. Or someone's. "I'll see that Jason never gets his hands on her again—or on any other mute. And I'll warn Coransee in case Jason finds a Patternist woman weak enough for him to abuse."

"All right. What else?"

Teray sat down and looked up at her. "I'm going to listen while you tell me about the other cases of this sort of thing that you've had to treat. Then when I've heard them all, I'm going to take a chance and pass the word that anyone who abuses my mutes will have me to deal with."

Amber frowned. "That's not taking a chance. That's your job. The only reason Jackman didn't do it was because he didn't have the strength to enforce it—or, as you said, the courage to go to Coransee."

"For me, it's taking a chance. You'll have to take my word for that."

She lifted an eyebrow. "In trouble with Coransee already, eh? I see. Well, I can't help there, but if you find that you need help with any of the others, you can call on me. I know you're strong, but you take away their fun, and they might not come at you one at a time."

She was abrupt and confusing. Teray couldn't decide whether to like her, tolerate her, or hate her. He was startled to realize that it was still possible for him to like her. He shook his head and smiled briefly. "Amber, why the hell haven't you gone out and started your own House?"

"I will, sooner or later," she said. "I just let Coransee sidetrack me for a while."

He hadn't asked the question seriously, hadn't expected an answer. But the answer she had given intrigued him.

"Are you an apprentice?"

"No."

"But you sounded serious—as though you intend to just walk away from Coransee's House someday."

"I walked in."

"Voluntarily?"

"Yes. He didn't have a healer and I didn't have a place to stay while I healed myself of some serious wounds the Clayarks had given me. I had just come down from Karston Sector. Then Coransee and I realized how well we got along, and I've been here ever since. But I'm not one of his wives, Teray, I'm an independent."

He had heard of such people—Houseless wanderers, usually possessing some valued skill that made them welcome at the various sectors. And possessing strength enough to make holding on to them not worth Housemasters' trouble.

"I didn't know there were any more independents. As bad as the Clayarks are now . . ."

"We're still around. We just stay in one place longer than we used to. We're still free people, though."

"I hope I'm around the day you try to leave Coransee."

"You probably will be. That time's coming fast. You know, we're supposed to be talking about mutes."

Teray let himself be shifted back. "All right. Tell what you know about mute abuse here in the House."

She turned and looked at Suliana. The mute woman seemed to be sleeping peacefully. Apparently Amber felt it more important that she rest than that she eat at once.

"Open," said Amber. "I'll give it to you all at once."

He was not completely comfortable opening to her. After all, if she had chosen to stay with Coransee, she must have felt some loyalty to him. But then, what could she pick up from Teray that Coransee did not already know? What difference did it make? He opened.

What she handed him made him feel as though he had suddenly been dropped into a cesspool. He digested the list of atrocities weakly, revising his thinking. He had thought Jason an animal for what he had done to Suliana. Now he knew that alongside some others, Jason could qualify as the House humanitarian. No one actually killed mutes, but certain of the outsiders and women made a grotesque game of coming as close to killing them as they could. Having two mutes fight each other, for instance, until one of them was so mutilated and broken that he could no longer control his body enough to fight on. Privileges and possessions were wagered on these fights. And there was a certain Patternist woman who had made an art form of controlling and changing the development of unborn mute children. Already she had created several misshapen monstrosities that had to be destroyed. She got away with what she did because infants and even older children, Patternist or mute, were considered expendable. Those who were defective in some irreparable way were routinely destroyed.

There was an outsider who had researched ancient methods of torture and made a hobby of trying them on mutes. Another outsider took sexual pleasure in stabbing a mute with a kitchen knife several times. And there was a woman who . . .

Teray shielded wearily and shook his head. "Amber, has this been going on while I've been here?"

"Not much of it. People know you're strong, and they're cautious. And too, most people repair the damage after they've done it—or they call me. But Jason had apparently decided that you're not going to be any more of a problem than Jackman was."

"How can Coransee let all this go on? He must know about some of it at least."

Amber looked away. "He knows. I've told him often enough myself. He won't let me do anything about it unless I give up my independence and settle here. I don't think he'll stop me, though, if all I do is help his muteherd avoid getting killed."

"But doesn't he care that his mutes are being tortured?"

"There's only one thing he cares about right now. And even though I understand his problem, it's driving me away from him."

"What are you talking about?"

"You ought to know better than I do." She looked at him curiously. "You're his brother. Jackman told everybody that. Full brother. I wouldn't be surprised to find you just like him—sitting around waiting for Rayal to die so you can try to win the Pattern."

Startled and suspicious, Teray spoke carefully. "I'm not after the Pattern," he said. "As I told Coransee, I want my freedom and a chance to establish a House of my own. That's all."

She looked at him for a long moment, one eyebrow lifted. "I think you're telling the truth. Which is surprising. Coransee wants the Pattern the way you and I want to go on breathing. It's just about that basic. If somebody stopped me from healing, I might be the way he is now—climbing the walls."

"He didn't seem that way to me."

"He can't afford to *seem* that way. But if you were a healer, you'd know. Or just if you'd known him longer. He does things to people now, or lets things be done, that he would never have tolerated two years ago when I met him."

"All because he wants the Pattern so badly."

"More than wants—*needs*. Holding the Pattern is what he was born to do, and it needs doing. He was all right when Rayal was doing an adequate job of holding it. Now . . . Rayal has all he can do to keep himself alive, and it might be better for the people if he didn't even do that. The people need a new Patternmaster, and believe me, it's a need Coransee can feel. But he doesn't dare do anything about it until Rayal lets go."

"You think you know a lot about it."

"I'm a good healer. I can't help knowing."

"If you're right, it seems to me there's not much more wrong with Coransee than there is with Jason and probably a lot of other people in this House. They're confined here together with people they're far from in the Pattern, and denied the right to do work that would have meaning to them—and denied a few other important things."

She nodded. "And you see what it's doing to them, what it's driving them to do. Think of the damage Coransee could do if he really gave way to his frustration."

"Don't think he isn't giving way to it just because you see him."

"You're still alive."

He jumped, and stared at her, wondering how much she knew. "All right. But if he can neglect his House the way he obviously has and allow the kind of perversion that goes on here, I'm afraid to even think of what he'll do if he takes on the larger responsibility of holding the Pattern."

"No need to be. Once he has the Pattern, once desire for it isn't eating him alive, then he'll be able to settle down and attend to the details of protecting and leading the people. The way he protected and led his House before Rayal's health got so bad."

"You're biased," he said. "You care about him. You can make excuses for him."

She shrugged. "Anything else I can tell you to help with your mutes?" She was getting up to go.

"No. I guess I'll get this one back to her room." He looked at Suliana, then at the meal he had ordered. "Shouldn't she eat?"

"When she wakes up. Why don't you keep her here? She's well enough."

"Mind your own business."

She laughed, then sobered. "Just keep her away from Jason. That will be plenty for me." She went out the door, leaving Teray staring after her, frowning. She was next to him in the Pattern. So close that he could have had a free, effortless, almost-involuntary communication with her. In fact, Teray had had to make a conscious effort to avoid such communication once he had accepted information from her mentally. Best to keep away from her. If he did manage to learn something that would help him against Coransee, he didn't want to inadvertently give it to her just because they communicated so easily.

He glanced once more at Suliana, then cast around the House for Jason. The man was in his room, sleeping peacefully. Teray headed toward his room.

Three minutes later, Jason was wide awake and protesting indignantly from the floor where Teray had thrown him after he'd dragged him out of bed. Jason was not hurt, not afraid. He was angry. Angry enough to lash out hard at Teray without first noticing what the Pattern could have told him about Teray's strength. He was strong himself, according to the Pattern; nevertheless, it would have been prudent for him to find out what he could about his opponent before he attacked.

But Teray had not wanted him to be prudent.

Teray absorbed the first wild blow and instantly traced it back to its source, through Jason's shield. Jason was strong all right, but he had no speed. Now Teray held him, left him no more control over what happened to him than he had left Suliana. Teray extended his own screening and enveloped Jason in it so that he could not call for help. Then, quietly, methodically, Teray held the man conscious and beat him. Beat him until he begged Teray to stop, and on until he no longer had the strength to beg.

Finally, Teray gave him a parting thought and let him lose consciousness. *Touch another of my mutes,* he sent, *and you'll find out just how gentle I've been with you.*

Jason passed out without replying. There was nothing permanently wrong with him, no physical injury at all.

But Teray had made certain that he suffered at least as much as he had caused Suliana to suffer.

Back in Teray's room, Suliana was awake and eating ravenously. She looked up, frightened, as he came in, and he smiled to reassure her.

"I thought I was going to have to carry you back to your room," he told her.

"I don't have to go back to Jason?" Her voice was soft, tentative.

"You don't have to go back to Jason. Ever."

"I don't belong to him anymore?"

"That's right."

She sighed. "Jackman said that once."

"I'm not Jackman. And after the . . . discussion I just had with Jason, I don't think he'll bother you again."

She looked at him uncertainly, as though she still did not know whether to believe him. He could have set her mind at ease immediately, simply by directing her to believe, directing her even to forget Jason. That was the way mutes were usually handled. Teray preferred to let her find out for herself. He found himself unwilling to tamper with the mutes' minds any more than he absolutely had to. They were intelligent. They could think for themselves if anyone ever gave them the chance.

"If I don't have to go back to Jason," said Suliana, "why can't I stay here?"

Teray looked at her in surprise, then took a good look at her. She was small and thin—too thin, really. But she had an appealing, almost childlike kind of prettiness. And there had still been no one since Iray.

"You can stay if you want to," he said.

She stayed.

He worried at first that he might forget himself and hurt her, but he programmed himself by his Jackman memories, made the restrictions of his self-programming automatic. Suliana enjoyed the small amount of mental stimulation that she could tolerate, and Teray enjoyed her pleasure as well as his own. He had not made love to a mute since before his transition. He found now that mentally and physically he had been missing a great deal.

The next day Suliana moved her few belongings to his room. Amber wandered up to check on her, saw that she was comfortably situated with Teray, and grinned broadly.

"Just what you need," she told Teray. "I thought you might take my advice."

"I wish you'd take mine and mind your own business," said Teray.

"I am. I'm a healer, remember?"

"I don't need healing."

She folded her hands tightly together and held them before her. "I hardly know you," she said. "But as you damned well know, we're like this in the Pattern"—she gave her folded hands a shake—"so when you lie to me, don't expect me to believe you."

She checked Suliana over briefly and went back downstairs without another word to Teray.

And as the weeks passed, Teray, in his enjoyment of Suliana and his new interest in his work, began to come alive again. Grudgingly, he admitted to himself that Amber had been right. In a way he had needed a kind of healing.

Now, healed, he began to think of leaving Redhill Sector. He would run away, escape to a sector where Coransee had less influence. He was not certain how much good that would do if and when Coransee succeeded Rayal. In fact, it might not do any good period, since Housemasters had a tradition of returning one another's runaways. And there was the even greater question of whether it was possible at all.

For as long as Teray could remember, travel between sectors had been too dangerous for a person to hazard alone. People moved in groups outside sector boundaries—groups of ten, fifteen, as many as they could. Even Amber, if she managed to get away from Coransee, would probably join one of the caravans of travelers that sometimes passed through the sector. But Teray would not be welcome in such a caravan. No one who knew Coransee would deliberately help a runaway from his House to escape.

Before the Clayarks gave their disease to Rayal, people had traveled freely, safely, from one end of Patternist Territory to the other. Even mutes had traveled alone, carrying merchandise between sectors and making their pilgrimages to the House of the Pattern. But now . . . In leaving Redhill, Teray might easily be committing suicide. But staying was surely suicide. Coransee might get tired of waiting and decide to kill him ahead of time if he stayed.

If he left, though, if he went to Forsyth, for instance . . . The idea seemed to fall into place as though there had never been any other possible destination for him.

Forsyth, birthplace of the Pattern, home of the Patternmaster. There was no way for Coransee to take Teray back from Rayal if Rayal could be persuaded to give Teray sanctuary. Surely the Patternmaster would resent Coransee competing for the Pattern while its present Master was still alive. In fact, Teray could even recall some kind of law forbidding such premature competition. If Teray could just get to Forsyth to plead his case. And at Rayal's House he could gain the knowledge Coransee was keeping from him. He could get training enough to make the outcome of his next battle with Coransee less predictable. If Rayal himself could not give the training, perhaps his journeymen would. Even they were highly capable people.

Teray began handling learning stones that told of travel, that revealed the terrain between Redhill and Forsyth. He memorized whatever he could find—memorized routes, memorized sectors that he would have to skirt. He could not memorize the locations of Clayark settlements because the Clayarks inside Patternist Territory had no permanent settlements. They were nomadic, roaming in great tribes, settling only long enough to strip an area clean of food. They had been known to eat Patternists, in fact. But a Patternist was an expensive meal costing many Clayark lives. The eating was ritualistic anyway, done for quasi-religious reasons rather than out of hunger. Clayarks consumed Patternist flesh to show, symbolically, how they meant someday to consume the entire race of Patternists.

· Four ·

A few days after Teray had decided to run away, he saw the Clayark. It was like a sign, a warning. Teray had taken several learning stones out far from the House to study in the privacy and solitude of a grove of trees. He had been so involved with the stones that he had neglected his personal security. There had been no trouble with the Clayarks within the sector since the day he left school, but still there was no excuse for his carelessness. To let a Clayark almost walk upon him unnoticed . . .

Normally, any Patternist wandering away from the buildings of his Housemaster's estate spread his awareness like a canopy around him. The moment that canopy—perhaps a hundred meters around—touched a human-sized creature, the Patternist was warned. Fortunately, Clayarks possessed none of the Patternists' mental abilities and had to depend entirely on their physical senses. Unfortunately, the Clayark disease, which so mutated human genes that it caused once-normal mutes to produce children in the familiar sphinx shape, also placed the minds of those children beyond Patternist reach. Only Clayark bodies were vulnerable. As Patternist bodies were vulnerable to Clayarks. Teray drew back farther behind the tree that had thus far concealed him from the Clayark.

The creature was a male, now standing on three legs and eating something with the fourth. Teray found himself watching, fascinated, comparing the creature to Laro's figurine. He had never had such a close look at a live Clayark before. And now that he was aware of the creature, aware that it was alone, it could not possibly act quickly enough to hurt him. But it was armed. It had the usual rifle slung across its back, the butt protruding over one shoulder so that it could easily be seized.

The creature threw something away, and Teray saw that it was an orange peel. Doubtless the Clayark had been stealing in the groves of Bryant, a neighbor of Coransee who raised fruit. The Clayark also had something that looked like saddlebags strapped across its back. The bags were bulging, probably with stolen fruit.

The Clayark was like a life-size version of Laro's figurine—well-muscled, tanned, lean, human-headed, and almost lion-bodied. It moved with the easy grace of a cat and wore a flaring red-gold headdress to make up for its lack of a mane. Being furless, it also wore clothing—the skin of some animal fixed about its loins, and another skin wrapped about the torso, probably to ease the strapped-on load.

But most unlikely were those forefeet that served also as hands. For Clayarks who bothered to wear running gloves of the kind that this one was now putting on, the hands remained supple and humanly soft. Clayarks who did not wear gloves developed the heavy callouses that caused the legendary clumsiness of the species.

Suddenly intensely curious. Teray checked the area once more, making certain that the Clayark was alone, then rose and stepped clear of his hiding place. A moment later, the creature saw him. It froze, stared at him.

"Kill?" The voice was deep and harsh, but undeniably human.

"Not unless you make me kill you," said Teray.

"Not kill?" The Clayark sat back on its haunches like a cat. "Why?"

"I don't know," said Teray.

"Boy? Schoolboy?"

Teray smiled grimly, reached out, and contracted the muscles of the Clayark's right foreleg. The Clayark gasped at the sudden pain of the cramp, half collapsed, righted itself, and glared at Teray in silent hatred.

"Man," said Teray. "So don't do anything foolish."

"You want?"

"Nothing. Only to hear you speak."

The creature looked doubtful. "Your language . . . not much."

"But you understand."

"To live."

"If you want to live, you'd better stop stealing in Red-hill. The Masters here are already after your people."

The Clayark shrugged. On it, the gesture seemed strange.

"Why do you raid us? We wouldn't kill you if you left us alone." He knew the answer, but he wondered whether the Clayark knew it.

"Enemies," the creature said. "Not people."

"You know we're people."

"Enemies. Land. Food."

It did know, then, indirectly at least. Clayarks always needed more land and food. They bred themselves out of whatever they acquired almost as quickly as they acquired it.

"You had better go," said Teray. "Before another Patternist finds you and kills you."

The creature stood up and stared at Teray for several seconds. "Rayal?"

For once, Teray did not understand. He frowned. "What?"

"You . . . your father. Rayal?"

Teray had the presence of mind not to answer. "Go, I said."

Catlike, the creature bounded off toward the southwest boundary of the sector.

Teray stood where he was, wondering how a Clayark had managed to recognize him as Rayal's son. Well, Coransee had said Teray looked like Rayal, and the Clayarks had gotten a good look at Rayal once years before. Some of them had even lived to tell about it. Perhaps one of them had lived to draw a picture.

Disease carriers that they were, they had deliberately mutilated Rayal, bitten him to give him the one disease that no Patternist healer could cure—the Clayark disease. Were they now seeking out his children, his possible heirs, to do the same to them? Was that why they had come raiding at Coransee's House to begin with?

Teray reached out, searching the direction in which the Clayark had gone. He swept the area, seeking, searching, but the Clayark was gone. That was one of the difficulties

Patternists had—not being able to reach Clayarks' minds. They could locate Clayarks only if those Clayarks were physically close to them—close enough to be touched by a spread canopy of awareness. Teray's canopy was much wider than usual because Teray was strong. The Clayark must have strained even its agile muscles to get out of range so fast. Teray wished he had killed it when he'd had the chance.

Hours later when Teray wandered home, he sensed something different about the atmosphere of the House. There were a number of strangers in the common room with the usual clusters of mutes, outsiders, and women. His first thought was that there had been some trouble with the Clayarks and Coransee had called for help. But things were too relaxed for that. The strangers were sprawled about, lazily resting, being entertained by a stone or a figurine, or trying to seduce members of Coransee's House.

Teray looked around the room and spotted Amber deeply immersed in the contents of a learning stone. He went over to her and touched her wrist lightly to make her aware of him.

She jumped, and looked around like a person just waking up. Then she saw him and put the stone aside. "I think you may have come home just in time," she said.

"Why? What's going on?"

"Your friend Joachim. He's brought one of Rayal's journeymen here. I don't think it was a very bright thing for him to do, but I think he did it for you."

He frowned at her. "Why would you think that?"

"You mean how do I know anything about it?"

"Yes!"

She hesitated. "Well, you might as well know. Remember that heart attack Coransee gave you on your first night here?"

He said nothing, stared at her in comprehension and humiliation.

"It's so much easier to hurt or kill than it is to heal," she said. "Especially to heal someone other than yourself. Coransee had to call me to save your life. I didn't ask any questions then, but I did later—after Suliana. And Coransee answered them."

Teray turned away from her in disgust. She caught his arm before he could leave, and held on just a moment longer than necessary. Communication flared between them, wordless, startlingly easy. No information was exchanged. There was only the unexpected unity, closer than Teray had ever experienced, and certainly closer than he wanted.

Amber took her hand from his arm, and the unity ended. It did not halt abruptly, but seemed to ebb away slowly until Teray was alone with himself again.

"I didn't ask him out of idle curiosity," she said.

It took him a second or two to remember what she was talking about. By then, he did not care. "Listen," he said, stepping back from her, rubbing his arm. "Listen, don't do that again. Ever."

"All right," she said.

She agreed too quickly. He did not trust her. But before he could reinforce his words, he received a call from

Coransee. He turned without a word and walked away from Amber.

As he went, he tried to shake himself free of the shared unity. He should have remembered his own resolution to keep away from Amber unless he needed her as a healer. What if she accidentally—or not-so-accidentally—picked up his plan to escape? But no, as he had gotten nothing from her, she had learned nothing from him. She hadn't been trying to snoop through his thoughts. He would have shielded against that automatically. She had been trying a little seduction of her own. He wondered whether she had heard his "no."

In Coransee's office, the Housemaster himself waited with Joachim and another man, who was built along the same solid lines as Joachim but who was several years older.

"This is Michael, Teray." Coransee gestured toward the stranger. "He's a journeyman in Rayal's House."

Still standing, Teray looked at the man, sensed in him solid strength, surprising nearness to Teray within the Pattern, and quiet maturity. The man could have been a very competent Housemaster on his own, Teray guessed. But apprentices in the Patternmaster's House often opted to stay on as journeymen and never try for Houses of their own. Apparently, they found prestige enough in being Rayal's officials. And Rayal, as powerful as he was, still needed powerful, impressive servants. Michael was easily both.

"Teray," Michael greeted quietly. "I have some questions to ask you. First, though, I want you to know what's happened. Joachim, who was your Housemaster for a short period, has accused Coransee first of illegally forcing you into his House while you were still under the protection of the school—thus, of trading in schoolchildren."

Teray winced inwardly.

"And second, of competing for the Pattern now, before the legal beginning of the competition—while Patternmaster Rayal is still alive."

"It's true," said Teray. "I was Joachim's apprentice—technically still in school. Coransee forced me into his House as an outsider so that he could keep me from competing with him for the Pattern."

"Why do you say he forced you into his House for that reason?"

"He told me that's why he was doing it."

Even Joachim looked surprised at that. "It's clear then," he said. "Coransee was competing for the Pattern ahead of time."

Michael looked at Coransee. "I could look into the boy's thoughts for verification, but I would rather not have to."

Coransee shrugged, almost lazily. "If you expect me to confirm all that, you're going to have to. It's true up to a point, of course. I did take Teray from Joachim. And Joachim accepted payment for him. He accepted a very good young artist I had just acquired. I claim that to be a legal trade."

"Legal, hell!" said Joachim. "There is no legal way to trade an apprentice."

"Why did you trade him then—if he was an apprentice?" It occurred to Teray that Coransee was at his most

84

dangerous when he seemed most relaxed. That was when he had a surprise waiting.

"You forced me to trade him," said Joachim. "I've told Journeyman Michael about the hold you have on me. It shames me, but it's a fact. I won't sacrifice Teray's freedom by pretending it doesn't exist."

"You sacrificed Teray's so-called freedom months ago, Joachim. You sacrificed it to your own greed."

"I will open to Journeyman Michael to prove that you forced me to make that trade!"

"Open. Journeyman Michael will see that I forced you to give up Teray—as I did. But I did absolutely nothing to force you to take payment for him. You could easily have given him up as I demanded, without taking payment, and then gone to Rayal to complain if you felt you had been forced to do something wrong. Instead, you made a profitable trade for a valuable artist. Now you come back trying to cheat me out of the price you paid for that artist."

Joachim stared at him incredulously, understanding dawning in his eyes. He rose to his feet. "You lying son of a bitch. You son of a whelping Clayark bit . . ."

Coransee went on as though uninterrupted. "Of course, only outsiders can be traded legally. And, Joachim, clearly, you did trade Teray. You accepted payment for him. How could you have done that if you honestly considered Teray an apprentice?"

Helplessly, almost pitifully, Joachim turned to Michael. "Journeyman, he hides his crime behind technicalities. Read my memories. See what actually happened."

Coransee looked at Joachim with something very like amusement. Then he looked at Michael. "Journeyman, what is the penalty for the crime I'm charged with? Trading children, I mean."

"The loss of . . . your House." Michael glanced at Joachim.

Coransee nodded. "A Housemaster who trades an apprentice—or accepts one in trade—loses his House. But, of course, a Housemaster can trade as many outsiders as he wants to." Now he looked at Joachim. "And certainly, any posttransition youngster a Housemaster picks up outside the gates of the school can be classified as an outsider."

Joachim leaned back and rested his head against one hand. "God, I don't believe this."

Michael's mouth was a straight thin line. "Lord Joachim, you made the charge. Is there any part of it that you want now to retract?"

Joachim gave a wild kind of laugh. "You're going along with him. You want him to get away with this."

Michael looked pained. "Lord, did you receive an artist in trade for this boy Teray?"

"I never would have taken him if . . . Oh hell. Yes, I took the artist. But look, I'll give him back if you'll just . . ."

"That's between you and Coransee if the trade was legal, Lord Joachim. Are you saying now that it was legal, that Coransee did not force you to take the artist?"

"Shit," muttered Joachim. "I withdraw the charge. That part of it anyway." He glanced covertly at Teray.

Teray realized at once that now was the time he could have revenge on Joachim if he wanted it. His own memories would prove that Joachim had traded away a man he had acknowledged as an apprentice. Whether Joachim had Coransee opened or not, Teray's memories would be enough. He could cause Joachim to lose his House. Not only that, but such an act might win Teray's freedom. Joachim would lose his House, Teray might go free, and Coransee . . . ? Certainly Coransee deserved far more than Joachim to lose his House. He might actually lose it for the less-than-one-year period that Rayal had left to live. Of course, within that period Teray would have the freedom to learn. He would be able to travel safely to Forsyth and study at Rayal's House. But for that possible freedom he would have to sacrifice Joachim. There was no way around that.

And somehow, in spite of his severely lowered opinion of Joachim, he could not quite bring himself to destroy the man.

He realized that Michael and Coransee as well as Joachim were looking at him as though awaiting his decision. He met their eyes for a moment, then went to a chair at one side of Coransee's desk and sat down. "What about the other charge?" he said disgustedly.

Joachim seemed to sag, eyes closed in relief. Michael was impassive, and Coransee seemed almost bored. He toyed listlessly with a smooth cube of stone—probably a blank stone with nothing yet recorded into it. Perhaps he was even recording into it now.

"The other charge," said Michael wearily. "Competing for the Pattern before the competition is open."

"I deny it," said Coransee simply.

Michael frowned. "You deny that you took Teray into

your House in order to keep him from competing with you for the Pattern?"

"Yes."

Teray sat up very straight, wanting to dispute, wanting to damn Coransee for the liar he was, but Joachim's fate had made him cautious. He waited to see how Michael would handle it.

"Teray," the journeyman said, "you say Coransee told you he meant to keep you from competing?"

"Yes, Journeyman."

"And how did he plan to stop you?"

"Either by controlling me as Joachim is controlled, or by killing me—if I refused to be controlled."

Michael turned slightly in his chair so that he faced Teray squarely. "Are you controlled, then?"

"No. I refused control. He's given me time to change my mind." Immediately Teray wished he had left off the last sentence.

"How much time, Teray?" It was Coransee who asked the question.

Michael looked at him in surprise. "Lord, are you admitting that you used such intimidation?"

"Yes. Though not for the reason Teray gives. But even if I had threatened Teray as he says . . . answer my question, Teray. How much time did I give you?"

There was no point in telling anything but the truth. It was in his memory—and he was not as good at twisting it as Coransee was.

"Teray?"

"You gave me as much time as Rayal has left, Lord."

"As much time as Rayal has left. And of course when Rayal dies, the competition for the Pattern opens."

Teray fumed silently, seeing the look of defeat come to Michael's face. The second charge had died even more quickly than the first. Teray let his mind go back over that morning, that breakfast with Coransee, trying to find some truth he could tell or twist. There was nothing. He himself could think of arguments to kill any arguments he might make.

Teray glanced at Joachim. "Thanks for trying," he said quietly.

"He's a hell of a talker," said Joachim. "Among other things."

Michael shifted in his chair, and said to Coransee, "Unless anyone has memories to the contrary, Lord, the charge against you is disproved. But there is something I would like to know for myself. Is Teray still under sentence of death?"

"He is."

"Why?"

"For the same reason Patternmaster Rayal killed the strongest of his brothers and his sister. Even if I win the Pattern, Teray uncontrolled could become a danger to me. He will submit to my controls, or he will die."

"I see." Michael lowered his head for a moment, then looked at Teray. "You don't have to answer me if you don't want to, Teray, but I'm wondering whether you think you might eventually be able to accept the mind controls."

"Not even if he was going to kill me right now," said Teray. "Especially not after this chance to see him in action." That was reckless. Teray wondered why he was bothering to talk recklessly while he was still in

Coransee's House. Maybe the Housemaster's lies had angered him more than they should have. After all, lies were what he should have expected from Coransee in such a situation. But Coransee had prepared for his lies long before he had to tell them. Coransee spoke quietly:

"Journeyman, if you're finished with my outsider, I'd like to speak with you privately."

And that simply, it was over. Teray and Joachim were dismissed so that Michael and Coransee could discuss more important matters.

In the common room, Joachim said to Teray, "I owe you thanks, too."

Teray shrugged.

"The trouble I went to to get that Michael here!" Joachim continued. "And then all the lot of us did was give Coransee a few moments of amusement."

"It doesn't matter."

Joachim looked at him strangely. "I'm more upset about this than you are."

Teray said nothing, his face carefully expressionless. He did not want to lie to Joachim but he could not confide in him. Joachim was Coransee's man, whether he liked it or not.

Joachim must have understood. He changed the subject: "What has Coransee promised you if you submit to his controls?"

"This House."

"This!" Joachim only breathed the word. He looked around the huge room. "He must be certain of winning the Pattern."

"I think he is."

"If you can resist this . . ."

"I can. I am."

"Teray . . . most of the time, the controls aren't that bad. And when he has the entire Pattern to keep him busy, he'll have even less time to concern himself with you."

Teray ignored him, and looked around the room to see whether Amber was still there. She had gone. Good. "Joachim, do you know a woman named Amber?"

"Teray, listen! You wouldn't be giving up as much as I did when I submitted. He's made me a kind of political puppet. But when he's Patternmaster he won't have to do such things with you. You'll be almost independent. And you'll be alive."

Teray shook his head slowly, eyes closed for a moment. "I can't do it, Joachim. I wouldn't be able to live with myself. A long leash is still a leash. And Coransee will still be at the other end of it, holding on. Now, do you know Amber?"

"All right, change the subject. Kill yourself. Yes, I know Amber. What do you want to know about her?"

Teray frowned. "Anything you know about her that isn't personal. She says she's an independent."

"She is. Strange woman. She's only four or five years out of school, but she managed to kill a man, a Housemaster, before she even made her transition. You ought to ask her about it. Interesting."

"No doubt," muttered Teray. "But look, how likely is she to go running to Coransee with anything unusual she hears?"

Joachim shook his head slowly. "Not likely at all. She likes Coransee, but she doesn't make any special effort to impress him. She does her healing and otherwise keeps out of House business."

Silently, Teray hoped he was right. It would be too easy for the woman to pick up something. No matter what happened, he was going to have to leave soon.

He found himself wishing he could speak privately to Michael, but he knew it would do no good. Even if the journeyman sympathized with him, the law really was on Coransee's side. Michael could not change that.

Journeyman Michael stayed two days more, then headed farther north on more of Rayal's business. North. Forsyth was 480 kilometers south. Teray could not even hope to catch up with Michael and try to attach himself to the journeyman's party. That might not have been a good idea anyway, though, since it would have meant asking Michael to risk his own life by defying Coransee. After all, if things went as Coransee expected, Michael would soon be under Coransee's direct control.

Teray would have to go alone. He realized that he was putting off leaving for just that reason—because the journey looked more and more like suicide to him. And what should he do about Iray?

That was something he did not want to think about. He was afraid to talk to Iray—afraid she might not want to leave Coransee, afraid her apparent interest in Coransee might be real. But even if it was not—she had kept her word, after all, she had not changed her name—how could he ask her to risk herself with him again? How could he take her out and perhaps get her killed? Then, strangely, it was Amber who gave him hope.

She was waiting for him in his room the night after Michael left. He walked in and found her staring out his window.

"Good," she said as she turned and saw him. "I've got to talk to you."

"You came all the way up here to talk to me?"

"Necessary. I have a message for you from Michael." And suddenly he was listening.

"Why would Michael give you a message for me?"

"Because I offered to carry it. He and I are old friends, so he trusted me. He couldn't very well give it to you directly."

"Why not?"

"God, you must really be preoccupied with something. Don't you have any idea how closely Coransee has watched you and Michael for the past two days?"

Teray went to his bed, sat down, and took off his shoes. "I didn't notice. It's probably a good thing that I didn't."

"Michael didn't think you would have lived long if he had shown any particular interest in you. There would be some kind of accident. You know."

Teray shuddered. He hadn't known. He hadn't even thought about such a possibility. It was true enough, though, that personal attention from Michael could lead to personal attention from Rayal. And surely Coransee would not want Rayal to have the chance to pay attention to another potentially powerful son.

"What's the message?" he asked Amber.

"That there's sanctuary for you at Forsyth if you can get there on your own."

In the moment of utter surprise that followed her

words, he did the thing he had feared he might do: He betrayed himself to her. His screen slipped—not far, and only for an instant. Coransee would have been hard put to read anything in so short a time. But Amber, it seemed, knew how to use her closeness to him. She read everything.

"Well," she smiled at him, "it looks like I've brought you better news than I thought I had. Just the news you need, in fact."

Teray dropped all pretense. Now, either she would report him or she would not. And Michael had seen fit to trust her. "What I really need," he said, "is a few good fighters to go along with me. I counted twelve women and outsiders traveling with Michael."

"Fifteen," she corrected. "Are you taking Iray?"

"I don't know yet. It seems to me—" He broke off and looked at Amber. She was still barely an acquaintance. Someone to sleep with, perhaps, but not someone to talk over his personal problems with. But on the other hand, why not? It was so easy. And who else was there? "It seems to me that I've done enough to Iray."

"I don't think you've done anything to her. Joachim has, and certainly Coransee has. But you're only about to."

"By leaving her—or by taking her?"

"By deciding for her."

"I don't want to get her killed."

Amber shrugged. "If it were me, I'd want to make up my own mind."

"I told her once that I wouldn't leave her here."

"Well, it's between you and her."

94

"Just out of curiosity, what are you trying to build between you and me?"

She smiled a little. "Something good, I hope."

"What about Coransee?"

"Yes." She took a deep breath. "Point to you," she said.

"What?"

"You remember telling me you hoped you'd be around the day I tried to leave Coransee?"

"You tried?"

"No. But I should have—some time ago. Now I've become a kind of challenge to him. Now I'm going to settle here as one of his wives whether I like it or not. He says. Which shows that he hasn't gotten to know me very well in two years."

"What are you going to do?"

"The same thing you're going to do. We'll live longer if we do it together."

He took several seconds to digest this. His main emotion was relief. "Two, or perhaps three, traveling together. That's better than one—though not much better."

"You're going to ask Iray, then?"

"Yes."

"Good. We'll need her."

" 'We.' " Teray smiled. "I wish you were just a little harder to accept."

"I'll wish that myself when the time comes for me to leave you. But I don't wish it now."

"You're staying the night."

"What about Suliana?"

"I just reached her. She's going to sleep in her old room—or wherever else she wants to."

"I'm staying, then."

She was a lighter golden color beneath her clothing. Honey-colored. The cap of black hair was softer than it looked and the woman was harder than she felt. He would have to keep that last in mind, if he could.

• Five •

Early the next morning, Teray left Amber asleep in his bed and went down to the dining room, where he had sensed Iray. He would assume that Iray had not changed. He would know nothing that she did not tell him. He would not prejudge her. She was eating with another woman and a man at the end of one of the long tables in the nearly empty room. Most of the House was not awake yet.

"I have to talk to you," he told her.

She glanced at him hesitantly, almost reluctantly. Then she took a last bite of pancake, swallowed some orange juice, and excused herself to her friends. She followed him out to the privacy of the completely empty courtyard where they had last talked. Since then, they had looked at each other, and they had refused to look at each other, but they had hardly spoken at all.

They sat down on one of the benches and Iray stared at her clenched hands.

"I'm sorry," began Teray, "but I have to ask you . . . .Is there any way . . . through you, that Coransee will hear what I say?"

"No," she said softly. "I'm linked with him, but only so

he can be sure that you and I . . . that we don't make love."

"The link is just an alarm, then?"

She nodded. "And I won't tell him anything you don't want him to know."

She was offering him the same loyalty that she had always offered, but somehow, something was wrong. Was it only her link with Coransee that had started her twisting her hands, that made her willing to look at him only in quick glances?

"Will you open to me?" he asked.

"You don't trust me," she said. There was neither surprise nor anger in her voice.

"I trust you . . . trust who you were. I want to trust you now."

"You can. I won't open to you, but I won't betray you either."

"Has he hurt you? Has he done something you don't want me to . . . ?"

"No, Teray. Why should he hurt me?"

"Then what's happened?"

"I took your advice."

There it was. All his fears wrapped in four words. He could not pretend to misunderstand her any longer.

"I started out playing a role," she said. "A hard role. Then . . ." She faced him, finally, wearily. "Then it got easier. Now it's not a role anymore."

Teray said nothing, could think of nothing to say.

"He's not what I thought," she said. "I thought his power had made him cruel and brutal, but instead . . ."

"Iray!" He could not sit still and listen to another

woman inventing good qualities for Coransee. Especially not Iray.

She looked at him solemnly, her shielded mind not quite hiding the fact that she did not want to be there with him. She had stilled her twisting hands, but her very stillness bespoke tension, withdrawal.

"Iray . . . what if there was a way out? For us, I mean. What if you didn't have to stay with him?"

"Is there?"

"Yes!" He had to trust her. How could he expect her to believe him if he did not tell her what there was to believe? He had failed her once. Twice. She had reason to be hesitant. He outlined his plan quickly, giving her the assurance that Michael had passed on to him through Amber without mentioning Amber herself. Now was not the time to cloud things further.

Iray took a deep breath and shook her head. "Clayarks," she said. "All the way to Forsyth. Hundreds of kilometers of Clayarks."

"Not that bad," he said. "We could make it. We could . . . ."

"No."

He was silent for a long moment. He could look at her and see that she meant it. Instead, he looked at the ground, at a wall of the House. "All right. I can't really blame you. I almost didn't ask you because I didn't think I had the right to risk your life as well as my own. And I don't have that right, of course. But I said I wouldn't desert you. I had to ask you if you wanted to take the risk."

"I'd take it. If I wanted to be with you the way I did once, I'd go."

He said nothing, only stared at her.

"You couldn't accept his controls," she said. "Even though your own freedom wasn't all that was involved, you couldn't accept them."

"Would you have wanted me controlled—like Joachim?"

"No! No, I understand what you did. That's why I never blamed you, never tried to make you change your mind. I knew you'd rather be dead than controlled. You did what you had to do. Then you told me what I had to do. And you were right both times. Well, now I've done what I had to do. And it was good, and I'm home. I'm going to stay here."

There was nothing he could say to her that would not twist back and indict him, too. Even his anger was more at his own helplessness, and at Coransee, than at her. He had thought of her with Coransee, even thought of her coming to prefer Coransee. But he had never really believed she would. In spite of all Coransee's power and apparent attractiveness to women, he had never let himself believe it.

She touched his arm and he savored her touch for a moment, then moved his arm away. She was still shielding him out and her touch brought her no closer to him. He could have taken more pleasure in Suliana's touch—the touch of a mute.

Or Amber's.

"Teray," she said softly, "I have to tell you—" She broke off suddenly as he looked at her. "I'm sorry," she said. "That can't mean much to you now, but I am sorry."

He stood up and started toward the common-room door.

"Wait!" She caught his arm again, this time in a grip

that he would have had to hurt her to loosen. He stood still, looking down at her, waiting for her to let him go.

"Leave soon, Teray, if you're still going. Soon. I said I wouldn't betray you, and I won't—not deliberately. But accidentally . . . Well, I'm with him a lot now, and sometimes he hears things I don't mean for him to hear."

After a moment he nodded and she let him go. But he stayed where he was, watching her, not wanting her to see the pain in his eyes but not able to turn away again. He raised his hand to her face.

She drew back from him sharply, then turned away and hurried past him into the House.

Teray stood still for several seconds longer. Finally he shook his head. He reached out to one of his kitchen mutes. The man whose foot he had healed. Silently, with careful gentleness, Teray gave the man orders. Then he reached a stable mute—a mute who was not one of his charges, but who, of course, was obliged to obey any Patternist. He gave orders to the stable mute, then went back up to his room.

Amber was dressed and having breakfast. Teray realized that he had eaten nothing, and at the same time realized that he had no appetite.

"When you get through with that, go get your things together," he told her. "We're leaving today. I don't want to spend another day in this place."

She looked surprised, but nodded slowly. "All right."

"And take as little as possible. Put some more clothes on over those or something. We can't go out of here looking like we're running away."

"I know."

"I'm having a supply of food packed for us and horses readied. And . . . there'll only be two of us."

She said nothing to that. She went on eating.

They traveled southwest toward the coast and toward the nearest borders of the sector. Teray had decided to take the coast trail south, if he could. The inland route was easier, less likely to be washed out or blocked, but it was also the most-often-traveled route. It was where Patternist caravans passed and where Clayarks lay in wait for them. The inland route was a little shorter, too, because it did not follow the eccentricities of the coast. But it did go straight through the middle of twenty-one Patternist sectors. The little-traveled coast route went through three.

There were some Clayarks along the coast route. But then there were Clayarks everywhere, breeding like rabbits, warring among themselves, and attacking Patternists. Teray hoped to find them only in small family groups along the coast.

Michael, he recalled, had traveled part of his way north along the coast route. Teray had asked a pair of his outsiders about their trip, prying as casually as he could. With his large party, Michael had had little trouble, but he had sensed at least one large tribe. He had gone into a Patternist sector to escape it. And that was something Teray could not do. He had a better chance against the Clayarks than he would have against a group of his own people who decided to earn Coransee's gratitude by capturing him. Until he reached Rayal's House, the only Patternist he could trust was Amber.

She rode along beside him, strangely accepting of his

surly mood. But then, she knew the reason for it. He wished she didn't. She said quietly, "I think we should link, Teray."

"What?"

"I know it will make us closer than it would make most people, and maybe you don't want me that close to you right now. But we'd be safer linked. If I sense Clayarks, I want you to know immediately—even if you're sound asleep at the time. If we don't work together, we don't have a chance."

"Oh hell," he muttered.

She said nothing else.

They rode for several minutes in silence. Finally, without speaking, he opened, reached out to her. Linking was like clasping hands—and did not require even that much effort. Now her alarm, her fear, almost any strong emotion of hers, would alert him. And his emotions would alert her. But beyond that, as he had feared, he was too much aware of the link—aware of a strong, ongoing sense of oneness with her. Normally, a link, once established, became part of the mental background, not to be noticed again until one of the linked people did whatever the link was sensitized to respond to.

But any kind of contact with Amber had to be different, had to be too close. There was nothing for him to do but accept it—and surprisingly, it was not that hard to accept. He felt himself relaxing almost against his will. Felt the anger and the hurt that Iray had caused him ebbing, not vanishing completely but retreating, shrinking so that it no longer occupied his whole mind. And Amber was not doing it, was not reaching him through the link to offer unasked-for healing. It was her mental presence alone that he was responding to. Her presence was eclipsing emotion that he would normally have taken much longer to get over, and he was enjoying it. He should have felt resentful at even this small invasion. Instead he only felt curious.

"Amber?"

She looked at him.

"What does the link feel like to you?"

She grinned. "Smooth. How else could it feel between people as close in the Pattern as we are?"

"And you don't mind?"

"No. And neither do you."

He considered that, and shrugged. He was too comfortable for her presumptions to bother him. He indulged his curiosity further. "All along you've known more about me than I have about you. Now I'd like to know something about you."

There was something guarded, almost frightened, in the way she looked at him. "What do you want to know?"

Her manner confused him. Apparently she had something to hide. But then, who didn't? "I heard you managed to kill a Housemaster even before your mental abilities matured. You could tell me how you managed that."

She sighed, and then kept silent for so long that he thought she was not going to answer. "It was an accident," she said finally. "The result of being a pre-Pattern youngster with no control over what was done to me. Who told you about it?"

"Joachim. He didn't tell me about it, he told me to ask you about it."

She seemed to relax. "At least. Well, the Housemaster

104

was my second and he shouldn't have been. From the beginning, we didn't get along. And because I was too close to transition to stand mental abuse, he used physical abuse—beat the hell out of me whenever he wanted to until one day I managed to push him so that he fell against the sharp corner of a low concrete wall. He hit it with his head. Died before anybody could contact a healer. Of course, my abilities weren't mature, so I couldn't help him."

"But none of that makes sense," said Teray. "Why didn't you tell the Schoolmaster that you didn't get along with your second? You could have gotten a new—"

"No, I couldn't. Like I said, pre-Pattern children can't control what's done to them. Leal—the Schoolmaster—knew he had given me the worst possible second. He did it deliberately because he knew I had already chosen my own second. And he did not approve." She gave a bitter laugh. "He would have seconded me himself if he could have—if he had been strong enough. He wanted to. He wanted a lot of things that a teacher can't have."

"You, for instance."

"Oh, he had me, for a while. For my last six months at school. I didn't mind. But we both knew he was going to have to give me up once I reached my transition. There was no way that I was going to be a teacher. Not with my ancestry. Leal could accept that, but he couldn't accept Kai, the second I had chosen. The second whose House I would have gone into. Although he might even have been able to stand that if I had been able to hide the fact that I was already in love with Kai. We met when she came to the school on some other business and Leal was the—"

"Wait a minute." Teray turned to stare at her. "She?"

"That's a good approximation of Leal's tone when he realized what was happening," said Amber. "I hope you're not going to react as badly as he did."

"I haven't decided yet," Teray answered. "Tell me the rest of it."

She stopped her horse, causing Teray to stop, then spoke very softly. "You'd better decide before we get into Clayark Territory," she said. "Leal's reaction almost got me executed. I'm not going to risk my life with anybody else who's that hostile."

The link betrayed her hurt. She had taken Teray seriously and was waiting for rejection.

"Do you feel any hostility in me, Amber?"

She looked at him mistrustfully, then read the message the link held for her—his lack of any emotion beyond surprise and curiosity.

She relaxed and they started forward again. "I'm touchy," she said. "Leal taught me to be touchy."

"Why did you tell me that part of it?"

"Because you would have found out anyway. Piece by piece. I would be thinking about it and off guard, and you would pick it up. We're going to pay a price in mental privacy for our closeness."

Teray nodded. "Well, Leal had reason to react with jealousy, but I . . ."

"Jealousy, anger, humiliation. How dare I put him aside for a woman? Poor teacher. He had trouble enough trying to compete with men for the women he wanted."

"I don't see why. He was the Schoolmaster. He should have been able to attract plenty of women."

"Yes, but not the ones he wanted. He could attract women teachers, but he considered them beneath his notice. He could and did attract older girl students, but they always had to either leave him or become teachers. He had the idea that women from outside the school were better. He tried to attract them—and usually failed. But until I met Kai, he had never lost one of his student girl friends to one of them. It was too much."

"And Kai even had her own House."

"Leal wouldn't have hated her for that if she had gone to him instead of to me. Prestige. But since she didn't, her House just became more fuel for his jealousy. He had always wanted a House of his own anyway, and he knew he'd never have one. He was almost too strong to be a teacher, but not nearly strong enough to be a Housemaster."

"A stronger man would have reacted more reasonably." Teray shrugged. "After all, you're not that unusual."

"Coransee didn't react too well."

He looked at her, startled. "What difference did it make to Coransee? It happened before you met him, and it didn't keep you from staying for two years with him."

"But it made a difference. I didn't tell him. He found out by snooping through my thoughts just a few weeks ago. That was when he decided that I was more of a challenge than he had thought. That was when he told me he intended to keep me in his House—deny my independence. Most people don't try things like that with a healer."

"Could he have succeeded?"

"Maybe, with his strength. Frankly, I'm afraid of him. That's why I'd rather run away from him than fight him."

Teray shook his head ruefully. "He has a habit of trying to domesticate people."

"What about you?"

"I'm still curious. I want to know how a pre-Pattern child managed not to be executed for killing a person as important as a Housemaster. I'm surprised that his friends didn't have you declared defective so that you would be destroyed before you gained your adult rights. And I'm curious about you and Kai. But all of that is your business. I don't want you to tell me because you're afraid I'll ferret it out anyway. I won't."

"I don't mind telling you, but that isn't what I meant."

No. He knew what she meant. "Last night I asked you what you wanted between us, and you said 'something good.' I think there was also the implication of 'something temporary.' That's all right for a start, but I might turn out to be as bad as Coransee. I might try for more, too."

She laughed. She had a nice laugh. "Don't do it. One Coransee was enough. Now I'll tell you the rest of my story. By the way, are you checking wide for Clayarks? I've seen them in these hills."

"Checking as widely as I can." They were just getting into the low grassy hills that they had to cross to reach the ocean.

"All right. I wasn't executed because Kai talked, bullied, and bribed some of the Housemasters of the sector council into voting to spare me. She didn't tell them anything they didn't already know—just that the killing was an accident, that I was only days away from my transition and my full rights as an adult, that the man I killed should never have been assigned to me anyway. They knew all that, of course, but they were so outraged, and, I think, so ashamed, that I, technically still a child, had managed to kill one of them . . . well they were more after vengeance than justice. The lead wife of the man I killed was there to goad them on. Leal was there telling as little of the truth as he could because he knew he was really to blame for the man's death.

"Kai got me off, but she couldn't get me all the way off. Instead of killing me, they exiled me from the sector. They meant for the Clayarks to do their killing for them. Kai was supposed to take me to the sector border and leave me there. Instead, she took me to her House. She induced transition—just a few days early, but early nevertheless."

Amber drew a ragged breath, remembering. "I swear I'd rather let the Clayarks get me than go through anything like that again. I kept trying to just die and let it be over, and she kept bringing me back. Did I mention that she was a healer too? Lucky thing. Although I didn't think so then. She dragged me through all of it—stripped away my childhood shield before I was ready to shed it. Left me mentally naked to absorb all the free-floating mental garbage within miles of me. I got other people's agony, violent emotions, everything, until I could manage to form the voluntary shield that I wasn't really ready to form yet. I almost killed her while she was trying to save me. I didn't know what I was doing. And I turned out to be stronger than she was.

"She pulled me through. But that wasn't enough. She had to prepare me to leave the sector—to use the abilities I barely knew I had. There wasn't time to teach me or time to do anything but print me with her memories. She gave me her fifteen years of leading her House. She made me assimilate all of it, not just let it sit the way you did with most of your Jackman memories. It was like becoming part of her—getting a whole new past that was only a few years shorter than my real past.

"She made me eat and took away my weariness and healed the bruises and sprains I had gotten thrashing around during my transition. Then she gave me supplies, put me on a horse, and told me to run. I got out just ahead of the group of Housemasters that had finally—twelve hours too late—realized what was happening."

Amber stopped talking and they rode along in silence for a while, urging the horses faster as they came to a stretch of level ground, then slowing to climb another hill.

"She loved you," said Teray finally.

"It was mutual. She almost lost her House because of me."

"Only almost?"

"She would have if it hadn't been for Michael. That's where I knew him from. She had called for help from Forsyth when I was first charged. Michael was in our area on other business but he had Clayark trouble on his way to us.

"He arrived and looked at my memories—I was allowed to come back into the sector to be heard. He looked at the truths the Housemasters had ignored, then decided in Kai's favor. He didn't make them take me back, but at least he made them leave her alone."

"It was too late anyway. You couldn't have gone back to her then."

"I know."

"With you stronger than she is and possessing so much of her knowledge and experience . . . I don't think she would have dared to take you back."

"I'm glad she didn't have to decide."

Teray changed the subject abruptly. "I think I've spotted some Clayarks." He hadn't had to say it. She was already looking off in the direction of the Clayarks. They were not visible, but there was definitely a group of them ahead, moving toward Teray and Amber. They were just beyond the next hill.

"Only a small group," said Amber. "About twenty. They might go around the hill and pass us by."

"Yes, and then they might notice our trail and follow us while one of them goes for reinforcements. Best to kill them."

"All right. You take it."

She opened to him as no one had since school, giving him access to and control over her mental strength. It was the way people who were close in the Pattern fought best. The way Joachim's House fought, the way everyone fought in war when Rayal used the power that he held. But only Rayal could pull all the people together, funnel all their strength through his own mind, focus it on Clayarks anywhere from Forsyth itself to the northernmost Patternist sector. Lesser people grouped when they could with whomever they could—with whomever they trusted not to try to make the control permanent.

Inexpertly, Teray channeled Amber's strength into his own. Then, almost doubly powerful, he reached out to the Clayarks.

The new strength was exhilarating, intoxicating. He almost had to hold himself back as he reached the Clayarks. Within one of them he located a large artery that led directly from the heart. He memorized its position so that he could find it quickly in the other Clayarks, then he ruptured the artery. The Clayark stumbled to the ground, clawing its chest.

Instantly the other Clayarks fled, scattering in all directions, but Amber, otherwise inactive, kept track of them, focusing and refocusing Teray on them until all were dead or dying.

Several minutes later they began riding past bodies. Amber was closed again—as closed as she could be while they were linked—and Teray had returned to her control over her mental strength. That strength was temporarily lessened, of course, as was Teray's, but the lessening was slight. One of the dangers of lending mental strength to another person was that the other person might use too much of it, might drain the lender to exhaustion and death. But neither Teray nor Amber was anywhere near death.

Teray stared at the bodies sprawled over the hillside, saw the expressions of agony on many of the Clayark faces, and did not know whether to feel sick or triumphant. Not one Clayark had had time to fire a shot or even get a look at the enemy who killed him. Still, Clayarks too were known to do their killing from hiding. It was strange fighting, repelling somehow.

"You've never done that before, have you?" asked Amber.

"No." Teray rode past a Clayark female, dead, with arms outstretched toward a smaller, completely naked version of herself. A relative perhaps. A daughter? Clayarks kept their children with them to be raised by the natural parents. Teray looked away from the pair, frowning. They were Clayarks. They would have killed him if they could have. They were carriers of the Clayark disease.

"I wanted you to handle it because I thought you hadn't done it before."

He turned to look at Amber almost angrily.

"I wanted to see you fight in a situation where there was no immediate danger," she said.

"Did you think I hadn't learned what to do back in school?"

"No, I was afraid you had. And unfortunately, you have."

"The Clayarks are dead, aren't they?" He was letting his disgust over what he had had to do spill over onto her and he didn't care. What was she complaining about, anyway?

"The last couple of them almost got away."

"Almost, hell! They're dead."

"If there had been just one or two more of them, we would have missed them. They would have been out of range before you could kill them. And sometime tonight or tomorrow, they would be back with all their friends."

"You're saying . . ."

"I'm saying you're too slow. Way too slow. A big party of Clayarks would swallow us before you could do anything about it."

"You could have done better?" Cold anger washed over him but his tone was mild, quiet.

"Teray, I'd be a little more diplomatic if it weren't for the chance of our meeting an army of Clayarks over the next hill. But to put it bluntly, school methods just aren't good enough out here. Will you let me teach you some others?"

"You want to teach me others?" he said in mock surprise. "Not handle the fighting yourself from now on?"

"Yes. You ought to have a chance to survive this trip even if something happens to me, or if we separate."

"And I won't without your teaching?"

"That's right."

"The hell with your teaching."

She sighed. "All right then, you owe me this much. The next Clayarks we meet, let me handle them."

"So you can show me how good you are at it. And I can change my mind."

"No, Teray, so I can be sure of us living at least that much longer." She spoke wearily, her words reaching him both through his ears and his mind. She was open again. And with his mind, he could not help but be aware of her absolute belief in what she was saying. In spite of her manner, she was not boasting. She was afraid. Afraid for him.

He felt the anger drain out of him to be replaced by something else. Something he could not quite name but that was far less comfortable than even the anger had been.

"Could you make it, Amber? Alone, I mean, from here to Forsyth."

"I think so." She was closed to him again.

"You know so."

She said nothing.

"You've done it before." ·

She shrugged. "I told you I was an independent. We travel."

"Why didn't you tell me?"

"Why should I have? The fact that I've done it before doesn't insure that we're going to make it now."

"Especially not with me acting as a brake."

Again she said nothing.

"We're about the same age," he said. "I'm the son of the two strongest Patternists of their generation, and I'm strong enough myself to succeed the Patternmaster. Yet here you are with your fifteen years of someone else's memories and your four or five years of wandering . . . ."

"Would you rather travel with somebody who was deadweight?"

"I just don't like feeling that I'm deadweight myself."

"Don't worry. With your strength, you aren't. I would never have invited myself along with you if I had thought you would be."

He looked at her sharply.

"No, that's not the only reason," she said, smiling. "You've got a few other good points."

He sighed, and gave up without quite realizing that he was giving up.

"Like your tractable nature," she said. "Open and let me show you how to kill Clayarks quickly."

He obeyed, watching her with the same mistrust that she had shown for him earlier.

• Six •

"You see," Amber was explaining, "we can't afford to waste our time and strength punching holes in the Clayarks. That's what they're trying to do to us with their guns. Fight them on their own terms and sooner or later they'll get you. There are just too many of them. In a large attack you'd have some of them blasting you apart while you were trying to punch holes in others."

Teray only half listened. His ears were full of the unfamiliar sound of the surf. He had spent all his life no more than a day's ride from the beach, yet he had never seen the ocean through his own eyes. He had seen it through the eyes of others in the learning stones he had studied, but that was not the same. Now, as he and Amber rode down toward the oceanside trail, he gazed out, fascinated, at the seemingly endless water.

He could see tiny rocky islands off shore. Nearer, the waves broke against sand and rocks with a noisy vigor that sometimes drowned out what Amber was saying. But that did not matter. She was only emphasizing the information she had already given him mentally. Mental communication detracted from their awareness of the land—and possibly the Clayarks—around them. Thus she was repeating, summarizing aloud.

"I can do it," he told her.

"Try it as soon as possible."

"The next time we meet Clayarks." But he was not eager to try her method of killing, or any method of killing, again soon. In his mind's eye, he could still see the Clayarks he had already killed. Maybe it would be easier if they were not human-headed or if he had not had a conversation with one. But she was right. He would not only have to get used to killing them, but he would have to kill more efficiently, in the way that she had shown him, if the two of them were to survive. He recalled the memory that she had given him of herself on foot, alone, running for the safety of Redhill two years before. She had been wounded but she had kept going. Her healer's skill had kept her alive and conscious. And she was still killing, limiting the area of her perception to a long narrow wedge, sweeping that wedge around her like a hand of a clock. The Clayarks she touched in the deadly sweep convulsed and died. By the time they were dead, she had swept over six or seven more. They had managed to shoot her by firing from beyond the range of her sweep. But such long-range shooting required marksmanship that not all of them—not enough of them—possessed.

Her sweeps turned the Clayarks' own brains against them. She used their own energy to stimulate sudden, massive disruptions of their neural activities. The breathing centers in their brains were paralyzed. Their hearts ceased to beat and their blood circulation stopped. They died, almost literally, as though they had been struck by lightning. Or as though . . .

Teray frowned. "You know," he said after a while, "your way of killing Clayarks isn't that different from the way we Patternists kill one another."

"It's not different at all," she said. "You just focus differently to kill Clayarks. You focus directly on the Clayark's body—his brain—instead of focusing on his thoughts."

"But . . . Then why do they teach us in school that you can't kill a Clayark the same way you kill a Patternist?"

She shrugged. "Probably because they don't know any better. Most Patternist nonhealers don't have any idea why other Patternists die when they hit them in a certain way. And they don't care, as long as it works." She frowned, and thought for a moment. "The focus is everything, Teray. Of course, we can't lock in on Clayarks the way we can on each other. We can't read their thoughts or even sense that they have thoughts, so we can't go after one of them the way we'd go after one of our own."

"What happens if you try—if you focus on a Clayark by sight, or you sense his physical presence and then hit him as though you were hitting a Patternist?"

"What would you be hitting?"

"His head, of course."

"I wouldn't," she said. "You might give the Clayark time to put a bullet through your head. The only people we can hope to kill by just mindlessly throwing our strength at them are mutes and other Patternists. With Clayarks, you have to know exactly what you're doing, and do it just right, or you'll get killed."

"A Clayark wouldn't be harmed at all if you hit him?"

"If *you* hit him—his head—with all your strength, he might have a seizure. But for most people, nothing."

Teray frowned, not understanding but not wanting to question further.

"Feel the wind?" she said.

"What?"

"The wind. There's a pretty good breeze blowing in from the ocean. There's a lot of power in the wind—even in a breeze like this. Ask Joachim. His House uses windmills. It doesn't usually seem like much power, though. Not until you find specific ways to use it, ways to make it work for you."

"I understand," he muttered.

"If I hit a Clayark as though he were a Patternist, he'd notice it about as much as you noticed the wind before I mentioned it."

"I said I understood."

"All right."

It was the disease again, blocking the way. A disease that protected its carriers and killed their enemies. The disease of *Clay's Ark,* brought back hundreds of years before, so the old records said, by the only starship ever to leave Earth and then return. A starship. A mute contrivance that had supposedly ended the reign of the mutes over the Earth they had sought to leave. That part of history had always held a grim fascination for Teray. His own race had been small then, scattered, disunited, a mere offshoot of the mutes. His people had been carefully bred for mental strength—bred by one of their own kind who happened to have been born with as much mental strength as he needed. One whose specialty had not been healing, teaching, creating art, or any of the ordinary talents. The Founder's specialty had been living. He had lived for thousands of years, breeding, building the people who were to become Patternists. Finally, he had been killed by one of his own daughters—she who first created and held a Pattern.

And meanwhile, mutes had been building a society more intricate, more mechanized, than anything that had existed since their downfall. Some Patternists refused to believe this segment of history. They said it was like believing that horses and cattle once had mechanized societies. But in Coransee's House, Teray had seen for himself that mutes were more mechanically inclined than most Patternists. And mutes were intelligent. So much so that Teray would have enjoyed challenging them—letting them have more freedom, encouraging them to use their minds and their hands for more than drudgery. Then he could find out for himself whether the inventive ability that had once made them great still existed. After all, even now it was the mutes who handled what little machinery there was in Patternist Territory. And the Clayarks, who were only physically mutated mutes, were said to use simple machinery in their settlements beyond the eastern mountains. On the western side of the mountains, however, Clayarks produced nothing but weapons and warriors. At least, that was all Patternists had ever known them to produce. Yet Teray found himself thinking about the Clayark he had talked to. The creature had known Teray's language, at least enough to communicate. But Teray, like most Patternists, knew nothing of the language the

Clayarks spoke among themselves. Patternists almost never let Clayarks get close enough to them to hear them talk. Patternists and Clayarks stared at each other across a gulf of disease and physical difference and comfortably told themselves the same lie about each other. The lie that Teray's Clayark had tried to get away with: "Not people."

That night another group of Clayarks drifted near them. Teray and Amber were camped on the beach, back against a hill. Amber had checked the horses over very carefully in what was to become a nightly ritual. She healed any injuries she found before they became serious, seeing to it, as she said, that they did not wind up on foot, and Clayark bait. They saved their rations and ate quail that Teray had mentally lured from one of the canyons in the hills. The Clayarks came into range behind them while they were eating.

Amber, aware of the danger the moment Teray sensed it, opened to offer him her strength. He accepted it, and used it to extend his range.

At once, he could sense the entire group of Clayarks walking toward them, moving through the hills rather than along the trail. Very shortly, those in the lead would see the two Patternists' fire.

Swiftly Teray reviewed the technique he had learned from Amber, then he swept over them like an ocean wave. A wave of destructive power, killing.

The Clayarks had almost no time even to scatter. The group was slightly larger than the one they had met earlier. But Teray handled it in a fraction of the time he had needed to handle the first group. He handled it using less energy, since he was not required to puncture or tear anything. And since he handled it so quickly, he did not need Amber to spot potential escapees for him. There were no potential escapees.

Since he would never see them physically, he swept over them once more to see that they all were dead. There was no movement at all.

He turned to look at Amber. "Satisfied?"

She nodded gravely. "I'll sleep better."

"You ought to pass your methods on to the schools—the one in Redhill, anyway. Save some Patternist lives."

"Healers usually stumble across it on their own. Most nonhealers can't learn it even with teaching. They have to either rip or puncture something, or they have to hit as though at a Patternist. My way is somewhere in between. I was afraid you wouldn't be able to do it."

"You didn't act as though you were afraid."

"Of course not. I didn't want you to try it with the idea that you couldn't really expect to succeed."

He looked at her, shook his head, and smiled slightly.

"Has anyone ever tried to make a healer of you?" she asked.

"They taught me what they could in school. I don't have much of an aptitude for it, though."

"So a lot of nonhealers told you."

"I don't, really. I don't have the fine perception for it. I miss symptoms unless they're really obvious. Pain, profuse bleeding, no one could miss those. But little things, especially things that are caused by disease instead of injury—I can't sense them."

She nodded. "Coransee has that problem, too, but you might not be as bad as he is. If you want to, when we get to Forsyth I'll try teaching you a little more. I think you're underrating yourself."

"All right." He hoped she was right. It would be reassuring to be able to do something better than Coransee could.

Travel grew more difficult the next day. They reached the higher mountains and found that the trail lost itself among them, "washed out, as usual," Amber said. The sectors nearest the coast were supposed to keep it clear, but during Rayal's long illness such work had become too dangerous. Teray and Amber walked and led their horses more than they rode.

On the third day they did no riding at all. There was no longer a beach. The waves broke against rocks and the rocky base of the mountains. They knew the canyons and highlands that they had to travel. These they had memorized. There was no chance of their getting lost. But they were losing time. Walking, scrambling over rock and brush, wondering themselves where they and the horses were finding footholds. The trek was physically wearing, but at least they encountered few Clayarks.

There were deer and quail for hunting, and there were cattle that they left alone. The cattle belonged to coastal sectors whose attention they did not want to attract. On the fourth day they traveled within the boundaries of one of these sectors. They passed through as quickly and carefully as they could. They were farther inland than they wanted to be. At one point they found themselves looking down on a large House comfortably surrounded by its outbuildings, which lay below them in a small valley. They hurried on.

It was while they were passing through this sector that they became aware of a great tribe of Clayarks. They were well out of sight of the House, riding easily now since the people of the sector took care of their part of the trail. But they didn't take care of themselves very well if they let themselves be invaded by so many Clayarks.

The Clayarks were resting—or at least they were not moving. Teray and Amber, their strength united, tried to find out how large the tribe was. They could find no end to it. It extended beyond their double range. Hundreds and hundreds of Clayarks; surely death to any but a large, strong party of Patternists. Teray and Amber detoured widely to avoid any possible contact with them. The Clayarks seemed not to notice, but neither Teray nor Amber could relax again for some hours.

Midway through the journey—on the ninth day rather than on the fifth, as it should have been—they had to leave the trail entirely even though it was well kept and smooth now. Here, it left the coast and ran through the middle of a large sector. It had only gone through an edge of the sector in which they had found the Clayarks. Now, though, the coast jutted out in a large peninsula while the trail continued on due south. Teray and Amber decided to lose a little more time and stay near the coast. They would not follow it as closely as they had, but they would stay well away from the Houses of the sector. As careful as they were, though, early the next day they suddenly became aware of Patternists approaching them on horseback. Seven Patternists.

By now Teray and Amber worked together almost instinctively, worked together as though they had been a team for months instead of days. And they both were strong. It was possible that together they could take on seven Patternists and have a chance of winning—if none of those Patternists was Coransee. Amber spoke as though on cue.

"I don't think any of them is Coransee. I only got a flash of them before I shielded, but I think I would have sensed him if he had been with them."

"People from this sector, perhaps," said Teray.

"No matter who they are, we're fair game."

The two groups met in a grove of trees, Teray and Amber on one side, and the seven strangers—four men and three women—on the other. Teray and Amber sat still, tense, shielded from the strangers, joined to each other only by the link. They waited.

"It would be best for you," said a small, white-haired woman in the center of the seven, "if you came with us without fighting."

The woman's hair was naturally white, not graying with age, yet Teray knew she was old. He could not have explained how he knew. Her age did not show in any definable way. Either she or her healer had stopped all physical signs of its progress, to leave her looking about thirty-five. Yet Teray had no doubt that the woman had lived more than twice her apparent thirty-five years. Which was unusual for a Housemaster—as this woman seemed by her manner to be. Most Housemasters were killed for their Houses long before they reached this woman's age.

"There are seventeen of us," the woman said quietly.

"Ten that I don't think you've noticed yet. We're all linked. Attack one of us, and you attack us all."

Immediately Teray and Amber became aware of the ten others approaching from the opposite direction, only now coming within range of the quick scan that they dared to make. Teray looked at Amber. Amber shrugged, then relaxed into a posture of apparent submission. What could they do against seventeen linked Patternists?

"What do you want of us?" asked Teray.

"To pay a debt," said the woman.

Teray frowned. "A debt to whom?"

"Unfortunately for you, young one, to your brother. To Coransee."

"You mean to hold us for him?"

"Yes."

Teray relaxed as Amber had, aware of the tension in the link between them. It was not the tension of a thing on the verge of breaking, but of a thing held in check, ready to spring into action.

"No," said Teray quietly.

The ten approaching Patternists came into view from among the trees. Teray ignored them, and felt Amber turn her attention to them, as he had expected her to. She was fast enough to sense any attack from their direction before it could do damage. Teray spoke again.

"If Coransee catches me, he'll kill me. So I don't have anything to lose in defying you."

"You have the life of your woman to lose. I can see that you and she are linked."

And Amber spoke up: "I'm not eager to have Coransee

catch me either. And I'm my own woman, Lady Darah. Now as before."

For the first time, the woman took her eyes off Teray. "I was afraid you might be. Hello, Amber."

Amber lowered her head slightly in greeting. "You're right, Lady. We are linked. We're going to stay linked. And you should be able to guess where we're going to direct all our power the moment you attack us."

Teray picked it up at once, suppressing his surprise that Amber knew the woman. "You know Coransee is my brother, Lady. That should give you some idea of my strength. Unless you're willing to sacrifice your own life as well as the lives of several of your people, let us go."

"I know you're strong," she said. "But I don't believe you could kill me. Not linked as I am with so many. If you think about it, you won't believe it either." She signaled the ten riders now waiting a short distance behind Amber and Teray. The ten began to move forward, clearly intending to herd Teray and Amber before them.

But neither Amber nor Teray moved. Through the link, Teray felt Amber's slight expenditure of strength an instant before he realized what she had done. Then he understood.

Six of the horses approaching them—the six closest—collapsed. Shouting with surprise, some of the riders jumped clear. Some fell. All seventeen Patternists had been expecting an attack on themselves, or at least on Darah. This attack on their horses caught them completely by surprise. Amber finished it quickly, giving them no chance to take advantage of the momentary opening in her shield. Teray was instantly on guard to stop any who tried.

But there was no movement other than that of the fallen riders and their horses picking themselves up from the ground. None of them seemed to be hurt. And as the Patternists remounted, none of them seemed eager to close with Teray and Amber again.

"Lady," said Amber softly, "you may have forgotten my skill, but I haven't. I can kill you here and now, no matter who you're linked with. I can kill you as easily as I'd kill a Clayark. I'm fast enough to do it to at least one person before anyone reaches me."

The woman held Amber's gaze steadily. "You'd die for it. My people would kill you."

"No doubt. But what good would that do you?"

"You're not under any death sentence from Coransee."

"No."

"And . . . in view of the favor you once did me, I might be willing to let you go. If you go alone."

"Might you?"

"Do you want to die, Amber?" The woman's voice had become hard.

"No, Lady."

"Then go!"

"No . . . Lady."

"I don't believe you're willing to sacrifice your life for him."

Amber smiled. "Yes, you do."

"And," the woman continued over Amber's words, speaking to Teray again, "I don't believe you're the kind to let someone else do your fighting for you."

"Do you think I'd be foolish enough to refuse her help against you and sixteen other people?"

"I just wanted to give you a chance to save her life—since you can't save your own."

"Lady, you choose any three of your people. Keep linked with them and sever with the others. I'll take the four of you on alone. That's the kind of chance I'd like."

The woman stared at him, then laughed aloud. "Boasting in a situation like this. You're his brother all right."

She didn't think he was boasting. In fact, Teray thought, in a way she was boasting—assuring him that he was doomed, yet not attacking. Trying to separate Amber from him.

"Are you ready to die now, Lady?" he asked.

She said nothing but her people looked more alert.

He nodded. "I thought not. I have no more time for you." He whipped his horse forward suddenly, sending it straight into Darah and her companions. He was aware of Amber moving beside him but he kept his attention on Darah and her people. Their horses reacted, leaping aside, startled, half rearing before their riders tightened controls on them, calmed them.

At a canter, Teray and Amber continued on, Teray now focusing his awareness ahead while Amber focused hers behind on Darah and her people. But Darah was not following.

Teray wanted to urge his horse into a headlong gallop, get away before the woman changed her mind. But he knew better. There was no "away" within his immediate reach. Darah could catch him if she wanted to as long as he was anywhere near her home sector. She had allies, no doubt—other Housemasters who would be willing to help her. And she had other members of her own House whom she could command to help her. It was all a matter of how much she was willing to lose to repay her debt to Coransee. He had no doubt that she was willing to sacrifice a few of her people. But apparently her own life was another matter. Now if only she did not find someone else more courageous—or foolhardy—to lead another attack in her place.

They rode on, no longer following their roundabout route, but traveling due south across the peninsula. It seemed better to take the chance of riding through more of the sector now than to take the time to ride around it. If Coransee wanted Teray held, then he was coming after him. He was probably already on his way, and possibly not far behind.

Teray and Amber had not spoken since their escape, but through the link, Teray could feel Amber's anxiety. She was as eager to put the sector behind them as he was. She was grimly alert, her awareness now mingling shieldless with his. Together they covered an area nearly twice the size that either of them could have managed alone.

With only brief rest stops, they rode on through the evening and into the night, not stopping until they had to, until both they and the horses were too weary to go on.

Then they camped in the hills, in a depression too small to be called a valley. It was surrounded by low grassy hills, so that while a Patternist passing nearby might sense them, no one who failed to sense them would see them and have reason to be curious. They lit no fire, ate a cold meal from the rations they had been conserving. Biscuits made that morning, water, jerked beef, and raisins. And for the first time they felt like the fugitives they were.

The night passed uneventfully. They slept as usual since the canopy of their awareness guarded them, once set, whether they were awake or asleep. The next morning they ate a quick skimpy breakfast and rode on early. They were no longer within Darah's sector but they were still close enough to it to be nervous.

A little of their urgency was gone, though. They reassured each other, calmed each other, without intending to. They had hardly spoken since escaping from Darah—had hardly communicated in any way beyond sensing each other's feelings. That had been enough until now. Now Teray was in a more talkative mood. And now he had something to say—perhaps.

"Amber?"

She glanced at him.

"Where did you know Darah from?"

"Here," she said. "The last time I came through, Darah didn't have a decent healer and she looked twenty years older than she does now. Of course forty years older would be more accurate. Anyway, I helped her. I had thought of her as an old friend. Until now."

"An old lover, you mean?"

She raised an eyebrow. "No. All her lovers are men."

He looked at her for several seconds, studying her. Golden-skinned, small-breasted, slender, strong. Sometimes she looked more like a boy than a woman. But when they lay together at night, their minds and their bodies attuned, enmeshed, there was no mistaking her for anything but a woman. Yet . . .

"Which do you prefer, Amber, really?"

She did not pretend to misunderstand him. "I'll tell you," she said softly. "But you won't like it."

He looked away from her. "I asked for the truth. Whether I like it or not, I have to know."

"Already?" she whispered.

He pretended not to hear.

"When I meet a woman who attracts me, I prefer women," she said. "And when I meet a man who attracts me, I prefer men."

"You mean you haven't made up your mind yet."

"I mean exactly what I said. I told you you wouldn't like it. Most people who ask want me definitely on one side or the other."

He thought about that. "No, if that's the way you are, I don't mind."

"Thanks a lot."

"You know I didn't mean any offense."

She sighed. "I know."

"And I wasn't asking just out of curiosity."

"No."

"You risked your life for me with Darah."

"Not really. I know her. She's managed to live as long as she has by gathering a solidly united House, and by avoiding situations that could kill her. She talks a good fight."

"She believed you were ready to die with me."

Amber was silent for a moment. Then she smiled ruefully. "I was. She's not only good at bluffing, but at seeing through a bluff, so I had to be."

"No, you didn't."

She said nothing.

"Stay with me, Amber. Be my wife—lead wife, once I have my House."

She shook her head. "No. I warned you. I love you—I guess we're too close not to get to love each other sooner or later. But no."

"Why?"

"Because I want the same thing you want. My House. Mine."

"Ours . . ."

"No." The word was a stone. "I want what I want. I could have given my life for you back there if we had had to fight. But I could never give my life *to* you."

"I'm not asking for your life," he said angrily. "As my lead wife, you'd have authority, freedom . . . ."

"How interested would you be in becoming my lead husband?"

"Be reasonable, Amber!"

"I am. After all, I'm going to need a lead husband."

He glared at her, thoroughly angry, yet still searching for the words that would change her mind. "Why the hell did you stay two years with Coransee if you wanted your own House?"

"To enjoy the man, and to learn from him. I learned a lot."

"You needed that on top of what you already had from Kai?"

"I needed it. I didn't want to be just a copy of Kai, running on her memories. Clayarks, Teray."

Her tone did not change as she gave the warning, but through the link he was instantly aware of her alarm. She had reason to be alarmed. She had sensed the edge of a vast horde of Clayarks—perhaps the same tribe that they had noticed days before. They were behind Teray and Amber, approaching from the direction of Darah's sector. It was possible that they had attacked one of the Houses there.

Teray and Amber had come through the hills to finally meet the old coastal trail, but the Clayarks were still in the hills. By the way they were moving, they meant to stay in the hills. There was game in the hills, and there were edible plants. The Clayarks were moving on a course that roughly paralleled the coastal trail. It was possible, even likely, that they would pass the two Patternists without ever seeing them. Unless they changed course. Or unless they spread out more widely. Or unless they had already seen Teray and Amber—spotted them from their higher vantage point before they blundered into the Patternists' range.

That last was a real possibility. Clayarks knew that two Patternists alone would not dare to attack a tribe.

"If they don't go any faster," said Teray, "we can keep ahead of them."

"I'm not so sure I wouldn't rather be behind them. I don't like the idea of their driving us."

"There are supposed to be some mute-era ruins not far ahead of us. Maybe the Clayarks will settle there for a while."

"I don't think so. I've been through those ruins. There's not enough left standing to give shelter to a family of Clayarks, let alone a tribe."

"That's not what one of the stones I studied said."

"Then that stone was out of date. I think people from

Darah's sector tore the ruins down because they attracted Clayarks."

That was reasonable. That was why most of the ancient mute ruins had been leveled over the centuries, at least in Patternist Territory. But he was in no mood to be agreeable.

"Maybe they'll stop there out of habit," said Teray. "Whether they do or not, we'd better keep ahead of them."

"Or find some cover and let them pass."

"No. If they get ahead of us and stop, they'll spread out. We'll have to detour back through the hills to get around them."

"Fine. At least we'll be alive to make the detour. If we stay ahead of them, and they decide to come out of the hills, we'll have nowhere to go."

She was at least partly right, Teray knew. She was always right. He was getting tired of it. "Listen," he said, "if you want to stay here and let them pass you, go ahead."

"Teray . . ."

He looked at her angrily.

"We can't afford this. Only people safe and secure in Houses can afford to let their emotions get in the way of their judgment."

"Do you want to stay behind?"

"Yes. But I won't. I'll stay with you unless the Clayark's start to veer in our direction. If that happens and you still haven't cooled off, I'll stay back and watch you go to meet them."

And that, he thought bitterly, was probably the closest

thing to a victory that he would ever have with her. Surely she had done him a favor by refusing to become his wife.

The Clayarks picked up speed a little and more of them came into range. Without thinking about it, Teray and Amber also moved faster. Then the Clayarks began to catch up again.

At that moment Teray realized that he and Amber were being pursued—or driven. Abruptly, there was no longer any question of what they should do. They had to find cover, a place from which they could make a stand. They could not outrun the Clayarks if the Clayarks were aware of them and intent on catching them.

Teray looked around quickly for a place where they could take shelter. Even as he looked, the Clayarks increased their speed again and turned toward the two Patternists.

Clayarks were, if nothing else, magnificent physical specimens. Running without restraint on level ground, they could reach speeds of one hundred kilometers per hour. Of course, they were running on hilly ground now—but they were running.

They were in a kind of flying wedge formation, and they were holding back, not running even as fast as the hilly terrain would allow. Even at their present speed, though, they could run down a horse. Left alone, they could race past the horses, stop more quickly than anything moving that fast should be able to stop, turn, and fire at the passing horse and rider. They had been known to do such things to mutes. More-daring ones had even been known to attack the horse and rider directly, leaping onto the horse's back or neck. They seemed totally oblivious to the risk to their own lives if they saw a chance to kill their enemies.

At a full gallop, Teray and Amber passed a grove of trees, ignoring them because they did not offer enough protection. There were rocks ahead, jutting up from the sand and continuing at irregular intervals out into the surf. Teray could see one place where they seemed to be high enough and wide enough to give shelter even to the horses. He directed Amber's attention toward it and left it to her to see that they got there. He turned his own attention back to the Clayarks.

With shock, he realized they were in sight. He looked back to verify the impression and saw them first as a line, then as a wave coming over the crest of a hill, far too close behind the fleeing horses.

He began to kill.

The first ones died easily, their legs collapsing under them. Their bodies, impelled by their speed, rolled over and over, tripping those behind them who did not see them in time, causing some to dodge or leap over the sudden tangle of bodies.

There was a sound like a baying of hounds, and the formation broke. Hundreds of howling Clayarks scattered, put distance between one another, some speeding up, some slowing, many keeping to the other side of the hill where they could not be seen, where most could not even be sensed. A few rushed completely out of the hills, speeding toward the two Patternists until Teray cut them down.

The shooting began.

The horses, sides heaving, reached the rocks, outran

them slightly, and twisted back as more shots rang out. Teray's horse stumbled and almost fell. He did not realize until he had jumped off that it had been hit. Even then, his attention remained on the scattering Clayarks. He was only peripherally aware of Amber beside it, cursing and apparently healing. It was a Clayark habit to shoot Patternists' horses since shooting Patternists themselves was not as immediately effective. A Patternist on foot was at least a slower-moving target.

Amber controlled the horses totally for a moment, made them lie down in the shelter of the rocks, then pushed them into unconsciousness. That was safest. It eliminated the possibility of their being frightened, or their bolting and being lost. Teray was aware of Amber shifting her attention, turning to help him. Then abruptly her attention was elsewhere.

He needed her strength to extend his range, to reach the Clayarks who had fled back into the hills and who were now trying to approach them, shoot at them from a better angle. They were managing to stay just out of his range. He looked at her angrily.

She was gazing off into space, her mind closed to him except for the link, and she was making no use of the link. He realized suddenly that she was in communication with someone. Another Patternist. Through the link, he received shadowy impressions of her fear, desperation, and hopelessness. Only one person could excite such emotions in her. Coransee.

He turned furiously and swept for Clayarks. He found only a few within his range, and those he killed instantly. Then he snapped back to Amber.

"How far away is he?" He did not want to reach out himself and touch his brother. That would come soon enough. That would come when for the second time he tried to kill Coransee.

"Not far. He'll be here in a few minutes." Amber's voice was soft, faraway. She was still in communication with Coransee. Teray seized her by the shoulders and shook her.

"Cut him off!"

Her eyes refocused on him sharply. She sat still, glaring at him until he let her go.

"If he's almost here, surely you can wait to talk to him."

Her gaze softened. She sighed. "I was trying to bargain with him."

He swept once more for Clayarks, and found none, but was now aware of the larger shapes of several approaching horses and riders. The Clayarks were leaving. Coransee had a party of about ten—ten, yes—of his people with him. Apparently that was more Patternists than the Clayarks thought they could pin down and kill. The shooting had stopped entirely.

Teray sighed and turned his attention again to Amber. "I assume you failed—in your bargaining."

"I think so."

He put an arm around her. "I could have told you you would. But thanks anyway."

"He wants to take you back alive."

"He won't."

She winced. "If we weren't so close, you and I, I'd try to get you to change your mind."

"No."

"I know. We're alike that way. Stubborn beyond any reasoning."

He looked at her for a long moment, then drew her to him. "Look, I want you to stay out of it when he gets here."

"No."

He pushed her away in alarm. "Amber, I mean it. He isn't Darah, to be frightened off. He'll kill you."

"Maybe. But he'll surely kill you alone."

He severed the link with her and almost gasped at the sudden terrible solitude. Solitude had never seemed terrible before. He had come to depend on the link more than he had realized.

"Teray," she pleaded, "please. This isn't an ordinary confrontation. He made you his outsider illegally. You haven't challenged him. You don't want anything he has. He's dead wrong, but he's still going to kill you. Your only possible chance is for me to help."

"I said no. He'll face me alone, without any of his people backing him. That's the way I'll have to face him."

She looked up at the riders now in sight, coming down the trail. "The hell with your stupid pride," she said. "You've forgotten that I don't want to go back to Redhill any more than you do. You'd better link up with me again, because when he hits you, I'm going to hit him. If we aren't linked, one of us is liable to get killed, without doing the other any good at all."

"Amber, no . . . !"

"Link. Now!"

He linked, furious with her, half hating her, feeling no gratitude at all. Pride. He was trying to save her life.

He stood up to meet Coransee and his people. Amber stood next to him, close enough to make Coransee aware that his arrival had not caused her to change sides. She was the one Coransee spoke to as he dismounted. He came up to them, but his people stayed back, still mounted, apparently watching for Clayarks.

"I don't suppose you persuaded him to submit."

"I didn't try."

"And you're staying with him. I thought you were brighter than that."

"No, you thought I was more frightened of you than that. You were mistaken."

He turned away from her with a sound of annoyance. "Teray . . . do you really want to die here?"

"I'll either die here or I'll go on to Forsyth. Nothing is going to get me to go back to Redhill with you."

Coransee frowned. "What did you expect to find in Forsyth, anyway?"

"Sanctuary." Coransee would find out sooner or later anyway.

"Sanctuary? For how long?"

"Even if it was only a few months, at least I'd spend them in freedom."

"You'd spend them learning everything you could to defeat me."

"Only because you've left me no choice."

"I left you one very simple choice and you . . ." Coransee stopped and took a deep breath. "There's no point in arguing that with you again. Whether you believe

142

it or not, though, I really don't want to kill you. Look . . . I'll give you one more choice."

"What choice?" asked Teray suspiciously.

"Not much of one, maybe. It's just that even with our ancestry, I find myself wondering more and more how much of a threat you could become."

Teray ignored the implied insult in Coransee's words. "Left alone I'd be no threat to you at all. I've already told you that."

"And it still doesn't mean a thing. It's not your promises I'm interested in, it's your potential, and that's something I can only guess at. Rayal would be able to do more than guess."

"You want Rayal to evaluate me?"

"Yes."

"What would happen if he found out that I . . . that I didn't have the potential to interfere with you?" It was a humiliating question to have to ask. No matter what words he used, he was really saying, "What will you do with me if I turn out to be too weak ever to stand against you?"

"What do you want to happen?"

"I want my freedom!"

"No more?"

"Freedom from you will be enough."

Coransee smiled. "You wouldn't ask me for more, no matter how much you wanted it, would you, brother?"

Teray said nothing.

"No matter. Are you willing to be judged by Rayal?"

"Yes."

"We'll go on to Forsyth, then. We're nearly there and I

want to see Rayal anyway. But there is one more thing. Only Rayal's findings can free you. You go to Forsyth as my outsider."

Teray shrugged.

"My property."

"You've captured me."

"Say the words."

Teray stared at him in silent hatred.

"I've wasted enough time with you, Teray. Say the words or face me now."

Say the words and give up any right to sanctuary in Forsyth, should Rayal's decision leave him still in need of sanctuary. Say the words that could later be picked from his own memory and used to damn him. Or refuse to say them, and die.

"I am your outsider," said Teray quietly. "Your property."

• Seven •

Time seemed suspended. The thirteen riders rode two
abreast with Coransee alone in the lead. Teray and Amber
rode directly behind him, still linked, but resting, no
longer watching for Clayarks. There were eleven others
who could watch. Teray felt his own weariness shadowily
echoed by Amber's. They had not let themselves realize
how draining the constant vigilance had been, especially
during the past twenty-four hours. And to have that vigilance end in capture by the very person they had endured
it to escape . . .

Teray looked at Amber, and read not only weariness but
bitterness in her face. He realized abruptly that the bargain
that he and Coransee had made in no way included her.
She had fled from Redhill because Coransee had denied
her independence, tried to hold her against her will. And
now she was his again. At least Teray had a chance for
freedom, but she was caught—unless she wanted to try
against Coransee her healer's talent for swift murder. And
she had already admitted that she was afraid of him.

Abruptly Teray urged his horse forward to pull alongside Coransee. He could not abandon the woman, could
not let her be drawn back into captivity without even try-

ing to help her. She had helped him. The shot rang out just as Teray moved.

Teray felt the bullet's impact so strongly that he slumped to one side, almost falling from his horse. He held on somehow, aware of pain now, growing, but oddly dulled. It was then that he realized that it was not he who had been shot, but Amber.

The link, fulfilling its function too well, had given him so great a share of her experience that if they had been alone he could have been shot too while he was recovering. But he was not alone.

He realized from the alert, intense expressions of the outsiders and women that they were already seeking the Clayark sniper. The party had come to a stop. Teray left the hunt to them, dismounted, and went to help Amber.

She had not fallen. She sat hunched over, coughing blood, fighting desperately to keep herself alive. She had taken a bullet through the throat. As Teray lifted her down she seemed to pass out. He felt the limp, dead weight of her and only the link reassured him that she was still alive.

He carried her onto the soft sand of the beach, put her down, and knelt beside her for a moment, wondering whether it would be dangerous to disturb her with an offer of help. Did she need help? A wound like that probably would have killed a nonhealer before anyone could do anything about it. She was not only alive but working to heal herself. Teray felt a hand on his shoulder. He looked up, startled, as Coransee knelt beside him.

"You looked as though you were just about to reach out to her," the Housemaster said.

"To help her. She might need it."

"No. I've seen her badly hurt before. She manages better if she's left alone."

Teray looked at him doubtfully, wondering whether he knew what he was talking about. But the link was no longer transmitting distress. Amber had gotten rid of her pain and she was no longer bleeding either from her neck wound or from her mouth. She seemed in control. Teray decided to leave her alone unless she seemed in trouble again. He got up, went to his horse, and got a clean handkerchief. He wet it from his canteen and brought it back to wipe the blood from her face and neck. Coransee watched him silently for a moment, then said, "Were you speeding up a little just before she was shot?"

"Yes, to talk to you. To talk about her, in fact."

"That's interesting. From what Lias said—she was riding just behind Amber—if you hadn't moved when you did, the bullet would have hit you."

Teray thought about that, and nodded slowly.

"It was probably you they were aiming at. You were lucky."

"Where was the Clayark?"

Coransee pointed inland toward the hills. "He was high and far back, but he waited until you and Amber were almost directly in front of him. I hope they don't have many rifles or riflemen who can make that kind of shot."

"Well, at least now they have one less."

"No. We lost him."

Teray stared at him incredulously. "All of you? You couldn't catch one Clayark?"

Coransee lifted an eyebrow. "That's what I said, brother."

Teray heard the warning in his voice and ignored it. "I don't see how you could possibly have missed him. So many of you . . ." He thought of something suddenly. "Lord, are you linked with anyone?"

"I'm not, but the others are linked in pairs."

And the range of a linked pair of them would be little better than Coransee's range alone. What good did it do Coransee to have ten people with him if he didn't use them sensibly? Teray found himself glaring at the House-master in open accusation.

"Blame?" said Coransee calmly. "What are we doing out here between sectors with the Clayarks, Teray? Why are we here?"

Teray made a sound of disgust. "All right, make it my fault if you want to. But you know as well as I do that you should link up with at least some of your people. You could stand it with a couple of them even though they're not close to you. Hell, you're the one who wants the Pattern. That will link you with everyone." He could see that Coransee was getting angry, but he did not care.

"You know," said Coransee quietly, "I would have stopped you some words back if I didn't realize you were speaking out of your feelings for the woman. But even for that, you've said enough."

Teray looked at Amber and saw that she was breathing normally now. For a while she had hardly seemed to be breathing at all. But she was pulling out of it. The wound was closed already. She was going to be all right. And this wouldn't happen again, because weary or not, he and

Amber wouldn't depend on the protection, the watchfulness, of others. They would look out for themselves as before, working together, their combined, extended awareness missing nothing. For days they had traveled safely alone. Now, amid a group of strong Patternists, the Clayarks had reached them. Coransee could not even be trusted to give protection to the people he claimed as his own.

Teray touched Amber's arm and knew that she was aware of him, that she took comfort in his presence. He looked at her silently for several seconds, then spoke to Coransee.

"You're right, Lord, I did speak out of love for her. I . . . do you intend to keep her?"

"Yes."

"I was afraid you did. If Rayal's findings free me, will you let me buy her?"

"Buy her with what?"

"With service, brother, work. I had planned never to see Redhill again if I was freed. But I'll go back and work at whatever you say if my service will buy her."

But Coransee was already shaking his head. "You're welcome to come back to Redhill, to my House, if you're freed. But she's not for sale." Coransee smiled slightly. "You'd never be able to hold her anyway."

"I wouldn't try to hold her against her will. I want her as my wife, not as my prisoner."

"You won't have her as either. At least not until I'm tired of her. But you'll have the same access to her as any other outsider if you return with me."

Amber opened her eyes and looked at Teray, then at Coransee. She did not speak. Perhaps she could not, yet.

"Of course," said Coransee to Teray, "you can have it all if you decide to stop fighting me. Amber will be the least of what you'll get."

Amber sat up, closed her eyes again for a few seconds, then opened them and stood up. Still without speaking, she walked over to her horse, took down her canteen, then went off several steps to a large rock. She leaned against the rock, kicked aside some sand, and vomited into the depression she had made. When she was finished, she rinsed her mouth, then took a long drink of water. She kicked sand into the depression, turned, and came toward them, eating something that Teray had not seen her take from her horse. Her eyes were on Coransee.

"I'm an independent, Lord." She spoke with slight hoarseness. "I'm an independent because most people realize how much trouble I can cause them if they try to hold me."

"You think I don't, after two years?"

"I think you haven't thought about it enough."

"That sounds like a warning."

"Good. At least you know me well enough to understand that much."

He hit her just as she was turning away. She shielded too late to escape the force of the blow. She fell to one knee, and stared her hatred at him.

"I've taken you into my House," he said. "You belong to me. You don't give me warnings."

"I'll give you this one!" Her voice was a harsh whisper.

"Hit me again and you won't have an undamaged organ left in your body!"

Teray came between them. He stepped between them physically, and emphasized the link mentally so that Coransee understood the situation.

"This is none of your business, Teray," said the Housemaster.

"Lord, she's just recovering from a wound that would have killed anyone else. Can't you at least wait until she's rested before you start on her?"

Amber came up beside Teray and said quietly, "Stay out of it, Teray. You've made your deal."

"Keep quiet." He didn't bother to look at her. Both she and Coransee ought to be grateful to him. He was giving them a way out. A way to avoid a potentially suicidal confrontation. Or, at the very worst, he was joining the confrontation and thus making it less certainly suicidal for Amber. "We're one," he told Coransee. "She and I are one. Attacking her is the same as attacking me."

Coransee looked at Teray with mild surprise. "She's worth your life to you?"

"She is." Not that he expected to pay with his life for siding with her. The moment of greatest tension had passed. Now Coransee would find a face-saving way out.

"Has she already agreed to stay with you?" the Housemaster asked. Had Teray succeeded where Coransee had failed?

"No, Lord. In fact, she refused."

Coransee laughed aloud. "Then you're a bigger fool than I thought."

Teray said nothing, stayed where he was. Coransee said

to Amber, "Would you let him throw away his foolish life for you, girl? You know I'd kill him."

Amber did not answer.

"You might even have some chance against me since I'm no healer. He'd have none at all." He sounded like Darah.

"Do you really want my life now?" Amber asked softly. "Are you trying to move him out of your way so you can kill me?"

He smiled. "I doubt that that would be necessary. Believe it or not, what I'm trying very hard to do is keep both of you alive."

"Then what do you want from me?"

"For now, a link. I want you to open and let me see what slowly lethal thing you may already have done to my body. Then I want a link that will let me know if you try to do it again. Only that in place of the beating you deserve."

"I'm linked with Teray."

"That's your problem—and his. To keep you from murdering me, I need a link with you. You warned me, after all. Refuse, and I'll have to kill you here and now."

She stared at him for several seconds, then looked at Teray helplessly.

"If you decide to fight, I'll stand with you," he said.

"No."

"We have a chance. Your strength coupled with mine . . ."

"No, Teray." She coughed and then was still for a moment, as though making some inner adjustment. "Not now. Not unless I have to, and especially not with you.

I'm too tired, drained. I might fail you." She hesitated. "Shall I break our link?"

"Break it? No, of course not."

"But you'll be joined with him through me."

"Only incidentally. He won't be able to read me any more than he already does. He and I are too far apart."

"But . . . he'll be more aware of you. You won't be able to . . ."

"Take him by surprise? I probably couldn't anyway. Besides, if you want our link broken, you don't have to ask. You can just break it."

"I don't want to. I should, for your sake, but I don't want to. I want you with me."

He only looked at her, loving her, wanting her, knowing that somehow he had to take her from Coransee. As he had to have his own freedom, he had to have her.

She turned away from the intensity of his gaze and he felt a flickering of fear in her. Fear of him?

A moment later she opened to Coransee. Teray had no awareness of the exact communication that passed between them. That they held private. Only through the link could he feel her fear suddenly expand, grow momentarily to terror, then lessen just as he was about to interfere. It lessened to anger, humiliation, hatred.

Then, as her emotions settled, Teray became aware of Coransee as a part of the link. The Housemaster was an intruder, unwelcome, bringing discomfort to the link for the first time. Teray tried to rid himself of the sensation of being mentally invaded. He knew that Coransee could not reach his thoughts unless he opened. Yet the feeling would not go away.

Teray ran his hand through his hair, wondering how he could ever learn to live with such a sensation. The constant feeling of being watched, spied on, by a hostile presence.

Amber, jaws clenched, caught his hand and held it. Teray realized how much more aware of the sensation she must be. She was linked directly. He was only receiving through her. Through his link, he offered her sustaining strength. After a moment of hesitation she accepted it.

With a start, he realized that she was near collapse. Healing such a serious wound when she was already so tired had weakened her greatly. And despite whatever she had eaten, she was ravenously hungry. He put his arm around her.

"Can we rest here for a while?" he asked Coransee. "You can probably feel how far gone she is."

"Is she?" Coransee glanced at Amber. "Tell him what you were going to do to me."

"What difference does it make? I can't do it now without alerting you ahead of time."

"I said tell him!"

She glanced at Teray, then looked down at the sand. "I was going to try to kill him tonight while he slept. The way we kill Clayarks. It might have worked if I could have caught him completely off guard."

Coransee nodded grimly. "Anytime you want to try your luck, healer, you can face me. But it will be face to face, with both of us wide awake."

She said nothing.

"Now, are you ready to go on or are you too tired?"

"I'm tired, Lord, but I can go on."

Teray started to protest, but the look Amber gave him kept him silent.

"Get to your horses, then," said Coransee. He went away, shouting to the others to mount up.

"At this point," said Amber softly, "I think he would have killed me regardless of the damage I'd do him before I died. Killed me and left me here. He's angry enough to take the risk. He still has the nerve to be outraged when he finds someone else trying to take unfair advantage."

"Would you really have done it?"

"Of course I would have done it. That's why he's so angry—and that's why he's more than a little worried. He's starting to think. He's thinking about how far he is from the nearest healer—other than me. God, I wish I didn't feel so weak!"

"I should have attacked him the moment I saw him."

"You haven't given up, have you?"

He looked at her, startled. "Of course not."

"Good. Because I think he's planning something for you. I got something from him while he was snooping through my thoughts. Not much, but it was hostile, and it was against you."

"That's not surprising."

"But . . . I don't know. It feels as though he's lied to you about something."

"About what? Letting me go on to Forsyth, or . . . ?"

"I don't know. I have to think about it more. I'll tell you as soon as I think I've figured it out. Hopefully, I'll tell you before I have to tell him."

Teray glanced back toward Coransee. "You think you'll have to open to him again?"

She smiled tiredly. "If you were him, Teray, would you trust me?"

They traveled for the rest of the day, Teray offering Amber as much of his own strength as she needed. She accepted only until she found in her rations enough readily edible food to steady herself. She refused Teray's offer of his rations.

"If that sniper is still around, you might wind up needing them yourself," she told him.

Teray's awareness of Coransee's link had dulled, was nothing more than an annoyance now. It kept Teray tense, made him do more looking over his shoulder than necessary, but that was just as well. The canopy of his awareness, spread as he had vowed it would be, covered even less of the area around him than it normally would have covered unassisted. This was not only because he had given part of his strength to help Amber, but because he was tired himself. He was worried about the Clayark sniper. If the creature fired again from as far away as he had when he hit Amber, Teray would have no chance of sensing him.

Then there was the possibility that Teray had not had time to think about. The possibility that Coransee had been more right than he knew when he suspected that the Clayark had been aiming at Teray.

They made camp that night against a long rocky ledge. They had not heard or sensed anything more from the Clayarks, but one of Coransee's women had sensed a doe back in the hills and lured it out. After everyone had eaten, Teray called Coransee aside.

The Housemaster had apparently gotten over his anger—or he remained angry only at Amber. He followed Teray away from the group far enough along the rock ledge to be out of earshot. There he told Coransee of the Clayark he had talked to before leaving Redhill.

"Lord, it recognized me," he finished. "It knew me as a son of Rayal."

"So you think the sniper today really was shooting at you specifically, rather than at the handiest Patternist."

"I think it's possible. And I think it might happen again—to either of us. After all, they've captured at least one of your mutes, so they probably know you're a son of Rayal too. They might even know just how near death Rayal is."

Coransee frowned, thinking. "They've captured more than one of my mutes over the years, but that last one . . . you're right. He would have had quite a bit to tell them. But as for the Clayark who identified you, you did kill it, didn't you?"

"No."

Coransee raised an eyebrow.

"I should have, but I didn't. No excuse."

Coransee looked away, exasperated. "You know, those four extra years in school didn't do a damn thing for you."

Without a word, Teray turned away to go back to the fire. He had delivered his message. Only hours before, Coransee had made a mistake that had almost cost Amber her life. A mistake that the Housemaster not only did not want to be told about, but that he had not yet bothered to correct. He had certainly not linked with Amber to widen the range of his awareness.

"Brother!"

Teray looked around at him.

"Back," said Coransee simply. As though he were calling an animal, Teray thought. Or a mute.

"Brother."

Teray trudged back.

Coransee leaned against the ledge, relaxed. "You will send the woman to me."

Teray stared at him, speechless, for a moment. "Amber?"

"Of course Amber. You will send her to me."

It was his right since he had claimed Amber. No woman of his House had the right to refuse him. His women could refuse any other man if they wished, but not him. "If you want her," said Teray, "call her yourself." Coransee could have called her without moving from where he was or saying a word aloud. But he preferred to humiliate Teray.

Coransee smiled. "She's less likely to do anything foolish if you send her to me."

"You're the one who's doing something foolish. You're pushing her even though you know that if she attacks you out here, miles from anywhere, you might kill her, but not before she's mortally injured you."

"I'm pushing her all right. I'm pushing you, too, brother."

Teray glared at him, hearing the challenge, ignoring it.

"You stood beside her today and tried to talk her into attacking me. You offered to help her. Do you expect me to thank you for that? If you were anyone else, you'd already be dead. Now go and convince the woman to come to me quietly—unless you want to find out just how badly I can hurt her without being hurt myself."

Teray completely surprised both himself and Coransee. He smashed his fist hard into the Housemaster's face.

Caught off guard, Coransee stumbled and fell to the ground.

Teray turned and, without hurrying, walked back to the group. He was tensed and ready to defend himself if Coransee attacked, but surprisingly the Housemaster let him go.

Amber was not beside the fire. He looked around and saw her preparing their pallet a short distance away from the others against the ledge. He went over to her and she turned to look at him apprehensively.

"I couldn't help feeling some of that through the link," she said. "From the emotions on both sides, I thought you two were going to have it out now."

"He wants you," said Teray tonelessly.

She was on her knees on the blankets, looking up at him. Now, after a moment of surprise, she rose and walked a few steps away and stood with her back to him. The contained fury he sensed in her alarmed him. He went to her and put his hands on her shoulders. She turned and was in his arms.

"I'd like to break his legs and leave him here alive for the Clayarks," she muttered. "I'm sorry, Teray."

"Sorry for what?"

"Sorry to be of use to him against you." Her voice grew bitter. "He doesn't give a damn about me now except to break me. He's doing this to humiliate you."

"I know."

"And that's not all he's doing. I finally realize how he was lying to you. I should have seen it from the first."

"Yes?"

"He's not taking you to Forsyth to be judged by Rayal. He's already judged you himself. He's taking you to Forsyth to kill you. He's as wary of you as he is of me, and he wants someone around to heal any damage you might do to him. Meanwhile, he'll make do with just humiliating you."

"You interpret the little you got from his mind to mean all that?"

"Yes. And it fell right into place. I know him, Teray. I know how he lies. You should, too, by now."

"But he could have killed me back at Redhill."

"Why should he have? You were still being a good, respectful outsider. Still doing as you were told. There was always the chance that you might come to your senses and submit. But then you had to go and run away—to Forsyth, yet, and with me." She took a deep breath, slowed down. "Well, think about it. I admit it's guesswork, but I couldn't be more positive that I'm right. If you decide you agree with me, you'd better start thinking about what you're going to do."

She bent to pick up a blanket. He caught her arm. They straightened, facing each other.

"You haven't said it all," he told her. "There's enough anxiety coming through the link to tell me you've left out something important."

Without speaking, she severed the link.

Solitude came to him jarringly. "Why did you do that? What's the matter with you?"

"You want me to stay linked to you while I'm with him?"

Understanding, Teray grimaced. For the second time that day, their extreme closeness made the link a handicap. "All right," he said. "You had reason to break the link. But you didn't break it soon enough. I know something else is bothering you."

"It's personal," she said. "My business."

From anyone else, that would have been enough to stop him. But he knew her better than he had ever known anyone else. He did not believe she really wanted him to stop.

"Tell me," he said quietly. He was still holding her arm and she wrenched away from him.

"You're as big a fool as I am," she said. "Looking for more trouble when you've already got plenty."

"What have you done that you consider foolish?"

She gave a short, mirthless laugh. "It's only my timing that's foolish, Teray. I decided that I wanted a child by you. And since I didn't know how long we'd be together, I didn't want to wait."

For a moment Teray's surprise left him without words. Finally, "You mean you're pregnant now?"

"Oh yes. And believe me, I wouldn't have told you if Coransee hadn't already found out. He realized it when he made me open."

"But you've opened to me and I haven't seen . . ."

"You don't snoop the way he does. It's practically an art with him. Open to him and he lifts your whole life."

"He's the last person who should know." Teray frowned. "Hell, he has the right to kill it if he wants to—

since he claims us and he hasn't given us permission to have a child."

"It's barely a child yet. It's only a few days old—just a ball of cells growing."

"You should have told me. I can't understand why he hasn't killed it already."

"I haven't let him," she said. "Because the way things are going, I wasn't sure you'd be around to replace it."

Teray winced. "That's encouraging."

"Just don't let him get you to Forsyth."

"How did you keep him from killing the baby?"

"I let him see how determined I was to have it. He decided to let me wait until we get to Forsyth, too."

"He told you he would kill it in Forsyth?"

"No, he withdrew without comment. He withdrew in that special way of his that means, 'Later.' " She sighed. "I think he only wants to kill it out of vindictiveness—because I refused to have a child for him."

Teray frowned. "I should let you know that I'm not ignoring the warnings you're giving me about Forsyth."

"I didn't think you were. You don't have to say anything more about it."

"Good. And I want you to know that I consider protecting an unborn child a responsibility for two. If Coransee reads that in your thoughts, fine."

"I'd feel the same way," she said softly, "if you and I had talked about it ahead of time. If we had both decided that it was a reasonable responsibility to assume at a time like this—which it isn't."

"No, it isn't." He hugged her and suddenly found himself smiling. "And I wouldn't have asked it of you until we were a lot more secure. But I'm glad you did it. Why did you refuse to have his child?"

"He waited too long to ask me. He waited until I had gotten to know him."

Teray laughed softly. She had given him a kind of victory. Not a large victory, but one he could savor. One that Coransee's humiliations could not destroy. And the child would be a living link between them even if Teray was unable to convince her to stay with him. Or it would be a part of him that survived even if Coransee succeeded in killing him. But he did not want to think about that last. Living suddenly seemed more important than ever. Living and keeping Amber and the child alive.

"Teray?"

He looked at her, knowing that she was about to leave him.

"What did you do to Coransee a while ago? I felt him almost lose consciousness."

He told her.

She smiled a very small smile, kissed him, gathered up a blanket, and went to Coransee.

we were a lot more secure, but that gave you—and it was to did you relax a little bit, didn't.

• Eight •

Amber returned to Teray before breakfast the next morning. She was quiet and withdrawn. She seemed to relax a little when he asked her to link up again. But through the re-established link he could feel her smoldering anger.

"Did he make you open again?"

"Yes." The anger flared for a moment.

"Are you all right?"

She did not answer.

"Is the child all right?"

"We're both all right . . . for now. I have to go back to him tonight."

Now Teray felt anger of his own. "If he's alive tonight."

"God!" she whispered. "Don't tell me anything."

"I don't know anything to tell you. I'm just waiting for my chance. He has to know that much already."

"He does. He knows everything I told you last night. He wasn't even surprised when he read it—and he didn't deny any of it. Look at him."

Teray looked toward the main group and saw Coransee standing encircled by his people. He was talking to them, and though Teray could not hear what he was saying, Teray felt suddenly apprehensive.

"We now have eleven enemies instead of just one," said Amber.

"Is he linking with them?"

"No. That's our edge. It wouldn't do him any good to link with them. He can't use a link for anything but an alarm. He's just ordering them to watch us. If one of us attacks him they're supposed to sit on the other one. That way, we can be almost sure that whichever one of us takes him on alone will be committing suicide. He'll be sure of taking someone with him even if he gets killed."

Teray nodded. "I can't blame him. That's what I'd do."

"*You* wouldn't hold free people prisoner and put yourself in the position of having to do it."

"Why can't he use a link with them—at least some of them—to borrow strength? I know they're not close to him, and it wouldn't be very pleasant, but he should be able to stand it. I could."

"If I had to," said Amber, "I might be able to take a few of them myself. But Coransee can't. He's too close to succeeding Rayal."

"What does that have to do with it?"

"He can't take strength from anybody until he can take it from everybody. I was with him the last time he tried, and I can't tell you in words how close he came to losing control. He almost made a grab for the Pattern."

"Almost provoked Rayal into killing him, you mean. Rayal isn't going to give up his power a day sooner than he has to."

"That's just it. When Coransee and I were on better

terms, he told me he would try to snatch the Pattern from Rayal if he weren't so sure of having it handed to him soon. But to get killed trying to snatch it away now would be worse than stupid."

"All right, so he can't use his people in the way they'd be most effective. All that means is that I'll have to fight him in the way I intended to from the first. Alone."

"Either you will or I will."

"I will, if for no other reason than that there are two of you."

"It doesn't matter much," she said.

He frowned at her, surprised. He had expected an argument.

"If you kill him, well and good," she said. "But I can feel that even you don't think much of your chances. And if he kills you, he'll still claim me. He'll kill our child and then he'll have to kill me. I'd rather be dead than be his property anyway."

She wasn't just angry, he realized. She was bitter and resigned. Her last sentence reminded Teray of what he had said when Michael asked him whether he could ever accept Coransee's controls.

"Listen," he said softly, "if I can't kill him, I'll cripple him. I'll hurt him as badly as I can. I'm not as quick as you are at that kind of thing, but I'll do what I can to soften him up for you. If you're able to break free of his people . . . you'll have an advantage." He wondered what the chances were of her breaking free of ten Patternists. They had to be far worse than his chances of killing Coransee. "I'm sorry," he said.

"Sorry for what?"

He did not answer. Their eyes met in understanding.

"He'll be watching you," she said. "Be careful."

As it happened, though, Coransee, like everyone else, was kept busy enough watching for Clayarks. The Clayarks were apparently closing in for the kill.

At least one sniper was with the Patternists constantly—sometimes more than one. The creatures kept out of sight, traveling through the hills. And they kept out of range—just out of Teray and Amber's combined range. It had occurred to Teray that one of the reasons Coransee still permitted him to link with Amber was the unusually wide range of their awareness. That and the knowledge that no other linked pair was as anxious about Clayarks, after what had happened the day before.

The group had come a short distance inland, crossing a small peninsula. In the clear air, they could see the ocean in the distance as they rode over a slight rise. There were Clayarks in the hills alongside them, firing uselessly. The Patternists had become used to them. But as the Patternists reached the top of the rise and looked down at the land and the vast expanse of ocean, a single deeper, louder shot thundered out.

One shot. Teray knew nothing more than that the sound seemed to have come from ahead of them, and that neither he nor Amber had been hit. He snatched more strength from her, reached, stretched, extending their combined perception as far as he could ahead of them, sweeping a wide area, finding and killing a single Clayark. There was only one in range.

Teray shifted his attention back to the Patternists and

realized that they had stopped. Coransee had dismounted or fallen from his horse. He was kneeling on the ground, Amber approaching him, others dismounted, going toward him.

Teray swung down from his horse quickly and strode over to the Housemaster.

"I'm all right," Coransee was saying to Amber. "I'm fine. Even I'm healer enough to handle this." He turned sharply as Teray approached. For a moment they stared at each other, Teray assessing the damage with his eyes alone. His mind was suddenly tightly shielded. Coransee said softly, "Try it, brother, and the Clayarks will make a meal of you."

Teray relaxed slightly, cautiously. Coransee's wound was not serious. The bullet had only torn through the flesh of his shoulder. He was not incapacitated mentally, not forced to give large amounts of his attention to keeping himself alive. He was no more vulnerable for his wound.

"You would have done it," said Coransee with surprise. "If you had come up and found me fighting for my life, you would have finished me off."

"As you would have finished me in the same situation, brother," said Teray softly. "I learn from you. And you have no idea what a good teacher you are."

Teray met Coransee's eyes levelly, but he was shaking inside with reaction to what he had almost done. And he was shaking with anger—anger at himself. He had been too obvious, in too much of a hurry. If Coransee had not turned and spoken, Teray might have made a fatal error. Inexperience. Never in Teray's life had he stooped to attacking a wounded person. He was surprised now at how ready he had been to do it. Coransee had indeed been a good teacher. But Teray found himself a little ashamed of having learned this particular lesson. He would do it again if he had the opportunity. But he wouldn't learn to like it.

Coransee seemed to read his emotion. The Housemaster smiled. "I see you surprised yourself too," he said. "You're shedding your school morality quicker than I thought. I'll keep that in mind." Coransee turned from him and began healing his wound.

Teray glanced at Amber and saw that she had been quietly surrounded by Coransee's people—just in case. Frustrated and angry, Teray went back to his horse and remounted.

"Where do you think you're going?" Coransee asked, looking up again.

"I killed the Clayark who shot you. I want a look at the gun he was using."

"Stay here."

Somehow, Teray controlled his temper. "Brother, by the sound of that gun, it wasn't the kind that the Clayarks usually use against us. It was something special, and if we leave it where it is we'll be hearing from it again." As Teray spoke, Amber went back to her horse, watched but not stopped by Coransee's people.

"You too, girl," said Coransee. "All this concern over a Clayark rifle."

"No, Lord," said Amber. "Actually, I just want to get away from you for a while."

Coransee stared at her coldly. "Go with him then. Be my alarm in case the gun gives him foolish ideas. Be my alarm and my eyes." He looked at Teray. "But don't even think about trying to get away again."

Without answering, the two urged their horses forward, away from the group.

"I should have followed through," Said Teray. "Even though he was ready for me. It has to happen soon anyway."

Amber said nothing.

"It will be harder than ever now." He looked at her. Her face was too carefully expressionless. "Whatever it is, say it."

"Just something you should be aware of."

"Yes?"

"You made a good kill just now, but you went after the wrong animal."

Teray frowned and turned to stare at her with sudden realization.

"I've never known you to move faster than you moved just now," she said. "You took strength from me, you hit the Clayark—nobody even knew what you had done until a couple of seconds after you'd done it. Now if you had forgotten about the Clayark and hit Coransee . . ."

Teray shook his head miserably. "I was responding to the Clayark," he said. "Not thinking, just responding. I don't think I could have moved as quickly if I had thought about it."

"I know. And he's not going to give us the chance to try it again, you can depend on that. The minute we get back to him, he's going to break us up. No more link."

"If he does, the Clayarks are liable to finish him for us.

None of his people can handle Clayarks as well as we can."

"Maybe. Or the Clayarks might kill one of us. We're only two days from Forsyth now. If I were him, I'd take my chances with the Clayarks."

They came upon the Clayark sprawled on the side of a low hill, his rifle lay beside him. They did not touch the weapon. Patternists had learned through bitter experience that Clayarks often booby-trapped their rifles just before using them—set them to inject a little recently taken saliva into the fingers of unwary Patternists. This could be done with nothing more than a few well-placed wood or metal splinters. Kept warm and moist, the Clayark disease organism could live for a few moments outside a human body.

Teray and Amber only observed that the rifle was not the usual Clayark weapon, as Teray had thought. It was heavier, and doubtless more powerful. Neither Teray nor Amber had seen one like it before. Mounted atop it was a telescopic sight that had already proven its usefulness. In the past, Clayarks had rarely used such things. But then, in the past, Clayarks had not shot Patternists from nearly a kilometer away with rifles.

Either the long period of Rayal's illness had given them time to improve their weaponry or they were simply bringing out their best guns—and their best marksmen— to kill two of Rayal's sons. Probably both.

"What shall we do with the gun?" said Amber. "Burn it?"

"Scorch it, you mean." Teray stared at the polished

wood of the rifle's stock. "There's not much more than grass around here to start a fire with. Mostly green grass."

"The gun has three bullets left in it."

Teray probed at the rifle where it lay, and sensed the three remaining bullets. He nodded. Then as Amber covered it with the driest grass she could find, Teray reached down to Coransee. He did not want contact with the Housemaster, but it was necessary. He found Coransee waiting for them, apparently finished healing his shoulder.

You're going to hear shots, Teray sent. *It will be us destroying the gun. Warn the others.* He was carefully open enough so that Coransee could see that he was telling the truth—that open, and no more.

Coransee returned wordless agreement.

Teray brought his attention back to Amber and saw that she was ready. She lit the grass, then both she and Teray took cover down the opposite slope of the hill.

There, while Teray kept watch for Clayarks, Amber saw that the tiny fire did its work. As the fire heated the metal of the gun's receiver, Amber extended her perception into the metal itself and observed minutely the reaction of the metal to the fire—how it changed as it heated. She claimed later that she had never examined an inanimate object so closely before. But she seemed to have no difficulty doing it. She observed the quickening motion of the molecules of the metal. And once she had observed it, understood it, she could control it. She could intensify the heat of the metal to a point beyond the ability of the tiny dying fire. For a moment she sweated, concentrated on doing the unfamiliar thing. Then the three cartridges exploded almost simultaneously.

The rifle leaped into the air with a roar. It fell to the earth in two pieces, receiver blown open, stock and barrel completely separated. The pieces landed heavily on the body of their Clayark owner.

Teray and Amber went down the hill to where they had left their horses and found that Coransee and the others had ridden forward to meet them. Immediately Coransee gestured Teray up beside him. He spoke as they rode.

"You know you're going to have to pay for what you did, don't you?"

"Almost did."

"Oh, you did enough. However clumsily."

"What do you want?"

"The woman has told you what I want. I saw it in your mind when you called to me a few minutes ago."

Teray looked away from him in silent defeat and desperation. As careful as he had been, Coransee had read him—had read him as easily as he had that first time months before on the day Teray left school.

"Break the link, brother."

After a moment, Teray obeyed and dropped back silently to his place beside Amber. Everything Coransee did made Teray more aware of how little chance he had of surviving a fight with the Housemaster. He had let himself hope, let himself forget. Coransee might make even quicker work of him this time, because this time the Housemaster would be out to kill instead of only to subdue.

Teray would die. Then Coransee would turn his attention to Amber. Eventually she would die. The embryo growing within her would die. Painfully, Teray considered giving in, submitting to Coransee's control. It was not something he would do to save himself. Could he do it for Amber's sake? He had not done it for Iray's, and Iray had been his wife. He thought about it, head down, perception indrawn, not caring at this point whether the Clayarks shot him or not.

No. No, that was stupid. Dying by a Clayark bullet would be the same as dying in combat with Coransee. Amber would still be left to the Housemaster. In fact, even if Teray submitted to Coransee's controls, Coransee would still be free to kill Amber. Teray would be of no more help to her than Joachim had been to Teray. Submitting would solve nothing even if he could have done it. And he couldn't have. He couldn't.

Amber.

What could he do to help her, beyond trying to cripple Coransee? And with ten Patternists restraining her, how could she get to Coransee if Teray did manage to cripple him?

He looked at her, then looked away. She was watching him. She was beside him, watching him, yet he had never felt so cut off from her. He could not link with her or speak openly to her. And tonight, against her will and his, she would again share Coransee's pallet.

Teray turned his thoughts away from that quickly. In that direction lay fury, recklessness, death. And he realized now more than ever that to be of any help at all to Amber, he had to find a way to keep himself alive. If there was a way.

Teray found himself thinking about Rayal. Journeyman Michael had promised Teray sanctuary if Teray managed to reach Forsyth on his own. How much of a difference would it make to Rayal if Teray reached Forsyth not on his own, but in tow, the acknowledged outsider of Coransee? Not a successful runaway, but an outsider. How much did Rayal care about either of his two strongest sons? He was the one man who could surely take Teray from Coransee if he wanted to. But would he want to? Apparently he had all but openly designated Coransee his heir. That was contrary to the law of succession, but who was going to force Rayal to obey the law? And if Rayal had chosen Coransee, why would he now oppose Coransee over Teray? But then, why should Rayal have offered Teray sanctuary at all? Would it be worth Teray's while to trust Rayal, go on to Forsyth, giving up hope of leaving a crippled Coransee for Amber to kill? If only he could reach Rayal and find out before he arrived at Forsyth. But he did not know Rayal. He had never had any communication with him, and never recorded within his memory the knowledge of anyone who had. That meant that he could not call Rayal as, for instance, he could call Coransee or Amber. It was possible that Amber had met the Patternmaster on her last trip to Forsyth and could share her knowledge of him with Teray. But Teray did not dare to ask her. Thus, there was only one way for him to reach Rayal. One illegal way.

Through the Pattern.

Since the Pattern connected each individual Patternist with Rayal, in theory, any Patternist, however lowly, could use it to contact Rayal. In fact, though, the use of the Pattern for communication was restricted to House-masters, Schoolmasters, Rayal's journeymen, and Rayal himself. Rayal, of course, could use it whenever he chose, but Housemasters, Schoolmasters, and journeymen were permitted to use it only to report a Clayark emergency. Lately Rayal had chosen to ignore their emergencies. It was possible that he would also ignore Teray's. He might even punish Teray for misusing the Pattern. But Teray had to take that risk. Had to take it soon—that night. Forsyth was getting closer.

That night when everyone was bedding down, Amber stole a few moments from Coransee and came to sit on Teray's pallet. She said little. She simply took Teray's hand and held it. The sensation was much like being linked with her again. Teray could feel her begin to relax. He could feel himself relaxing. He had not realized how tense he was.

Then a woman named Rain came over with a message for Amber. "He wants you."

Amber winced, got up, and left. Rain stayed a little longer.

"I was who he spent most of his nights with before we caught up with you," she told Teray. "You don't look any happier about being alone than I am."

Teray looked up at her and forced himself to smile. It wasn't hard. She was a beautiful woman, well-shaped, smooth-skinned, with a long mane of black hair hanging loose down her back. Another time, under other circum-stances . . ."I don't like it," he said. "But it's best. I'm too surly now to be anything but alone."

"Are you that tied to her?" Rain smiled and sat down

where Amber had been. "Give her a few minutes and she won't be thinking about anything but him."

"Rain." Teray held on to the shreds of his temper.

"So it seems only fair that you should have someone else to think about too."

"Rain!"

She jumped, and looked at him.

"Get away from me."

She was not accustomed to being refused. She flushed deeply and muttered something that was probably insulting, though Teray hardly heard. Then she stalked away angrily. Beyond being glad that she had gone, Teray did not care. Without moving, he closed his eyes and focused his awareness on the Pattern.

He had been lying on his back, looking up at the stars. Focusing on the Pattern now was like shifting to view another night sky within his own head. A mental universe. Other Patternists were seen as points of light constantly changing in shape, color, and size, reacting as individual Patternists changed their thoughts, their emotions, their actions. When a Patternist died, a point of light blinked out.

Teray, seemingly bodiless, only a point of light himself in this mental universe, discovered that he could change his point of view without seeming to move. He was suddenly able to see the members of the Pattern not as starlike points of light but as luminescent threads. He could see where the threads wound together into slender cords, into ropes, into great cables. He could see where the cables joined, where they coiled and twisted together to form a vast sphere of brilliance, a core of light that was like a sun formed of many suns. That core where all the people came together was Rayal.

Because Teray was doing something he had never done before, he first had difficulty understanding that the sphere of light was not a thing that he had to travel to, but a thing that he was a part of. He could not travel along the thread of himself. He was that thread. Or at best, that thread was a kind of mental limb, a mental hand that Teray discovered possessed a strong instinctive ability to grasp and hold. Teray grasped.

And instantly, he was grasped.

He struggled reflexively, uselessly, for a moment, then forced himself calm. He was not being hurt or even roughly handled. He was simply held in a grip that he knew he could not break. Something was done to him. He was disoriented for a moment, then he lost his focus on the Pattern and found himself channeled through to Rayal as though to a friend—as though he had simply reached out to the Patternmaster. And he was no longer held. He could break the contact if he wished.

The Pattern was again clear for emergency calls. Teray waited, giving Rayal access to his thoughts so that the Patternmaster could see and understand the situation quickly. It seemed to Teray that Rayal examined his thoughts longer than necessary, but there was nothing he could do about it. He was in no position to rush the old man. Finally, though, he became aware of Rayal sending.

Things have gone too far, young one.

Too far?

You're going to have to face him.

You mean you won't give me sanctuary? Not even

for . . . Teray caught himself, stopped the thought. But Rayal guessed what his words would have been anyway.

Not even for the time I have left? That's right, young one, I won't give you sanctuary for even that long. It wouldn't do you any good.

It would keep me alive! Me, Amber, our child. I'd have time to learn the kind of fighting that they don't teach in school.

You've had time.

In Coransee's House! Do you think anyone there would dare teach me what I need to know?

Rayal gave a mental shrug. *You've learned enough.*

I've learned nothing! You offered me sanctuary through your journeyman. Why are you turning your back on me now that I've almost reached you?

You know why. I offered you sanctuary if you could make it here on your own. Obviously, you couldn't; you were caught.

That doesn't have to mean anything to you if you want to help me.

It means a great deal. Especially since if you hadn't been caught, you would probably have been killed by Clayarks. Don't you think I had a reason for making your sanctuary conditional—for making it a thing you had to earn?

Teray was beginning to understand. He had been tested, and as far as Rayal was concerned, had been found wanting. That apparently made him not worth bothering about.

Can you . . . will you help Amber? he asked. *I'll let myself be brought into Forsyth, fight him there, if you'll give her sanctuary.*

No.

The thought was like a stone. There was nothing more to be said. Teray could feel the old man's absolute inflexibility. Teray shot him a wordless obscenity and broke contact.

Rayal was old and sick and useless. He had not fulfilled his responsibilities to the people for years. Teray was not really surprised to find him unwilling to go a little out of his way to help only one person. Especially when he might be helping that one to defeat Coransee. Teray still could not see why Rayal had bothered to offer sanctuary at all. Why even waste time testing Teray when he had already chosen Coransee to succeed him?

Teray sighed, opened his eyes, and looked around the camp. Apparently no one had detected his communication with Rayal. The camp was as it had been before Teray closed his eyes. He closed his eyes again, resolving to sleep one more night, live at least part of one more day before he challenged Coransee. He would not ride into Forsyth with the Housemaster. He would not give his life away. Tomorrow perhaps the Clayarks would give him another chance at Coransee. If they did, he would make good use of it this time. But whether they did or not, no matter what it cost him, he would do his best to spare the people the burden of Coransee's leadership.

• Nine •

The next day Clayark snipers harassed the Patternists from the moment the Patternists broke camp. The snipers kept well out of the Patternists' range and fired their rifles more to keep the Patternists on edge than to kill. It was possible that Teray's kill the day before had made them cautious. Which was just as well since Teray could never make such a long-distance kill now, alone.

Only once did the Clayarks become careless. A trio of them lying in wait let the Patternists get too close. Coransee spotted them first. He killed all three almost before Teray was aware of them—certainly before Teray could take advantage of Coransee's momentarily diverted attention.

Or rather, Coransee injured all three Clayarks.

Surprisingly, he fought Clayarks in the way Teray had before he'd learned Amber's way. He killed by imitating the action of a bullet and damaging Clayarks' vital organs. But he did it with blinding speed. He jumped from one mortally wounded Clayark to another, working as quickly in his way as Teray or Amber could have in theirs. Coransee's Clayarks took several seconds or even several minutes to die. But once he wounded them, they were helpless. His method denied the merciful quick death of Amber's, but it was just as effective.

The Clayarks apparently took Coransee's kill as a warning. No more of them came into range. They stayed well back and made noise. There seemed to be more of them now, shooting their guns at odd moments, sometimes singly, and sometimes in such large numbers that they sounded like a battle in progress all by themselves.

The Patternists' horses were skittish and had to be controlled more closely than usual. The Patternists themselves were skittish, first wearing themselves out seeking what was beyond their reach, then resolving to be content with what they could reach and assume that they were safe. But of course they were not safe. They could not know when the next Clayark with a special rifle would announce himself by killing someone.

The land around Forsyth had once contained a huge population of mutes. Mutes who had lived packed together in great cities. Clusters of the buildings left over from those cities still stood, in spite of centuries of Patternist demolition efforts. Nowadays, as Rayal conserved his power and kept himself alive, Clayarks did not just frequent these ruins. They gave up their wandering and lived in them full time. The Clayarks who had been harassing Coransee's party picked up local support. A young outsider named Goran—who happened to be riding directly behind Teray—had his horse shot from under him. Another special rifle. The sniper got away.

Amber could have saved the horse, but Coransee ordered it abandoned. He was in a hurry. He ordered Goran to ride with Lias, the woman with whom Goran usually paired.

As the group rode on, Teray saw Amber turn and look back. He realized that she had reached back and killed the wounded horse. He found himself wondering whether Coransee would have abandoned a wounded Patternist as easily as he had abandoned the horse. Why not?

The thought bothered Teray enough so that amid a nerve-shattering but otherwise ineffective volley of shots, he rode close to Amber and spoke to her.

"Keep your eyes open. I have a feeling we're going to have to take shelter sooner or later. And we're not going to have time to look around for it when we need it."

She nodded. "You think they're going to try to pin us down, then?"

"I'm sure they are. They know by now that we're not a linked group. We can't just reach out and send all of them to the hell they believe in. They want Coransee and me." He had told her about his talk with the Clayark. "And they know they're numerous enough now to take us—along with any other Patternists they can reach, of course."

"If you're right, they must have an ambush planned somewhere ahead."

"Either that or they're just trying to work up enough nerve to come and get us. It won't be easy for them even though we aren't linked. An awful lot of them will die whether they get us or not."

She said nothing for a long moment. Then finally, "There are some ruined buildings ahead. Just around the bend. No Clayarks inside—no sign of their having been inside recently."

Teray probed ahead and found the ruins. "Good. That's the kind of thing we'll need. I'll look too. It might be better to use your eyes, though. You'll need all the rest of your awareness for the Clayarks."

"I can manage both."

He glanced at her. She probably could with her healer's propensity for poking around inside and outside of things. Fine.

A moment later, as they rounded a bend, they came within sight of the ruins Amber had spotted. These were just the shells of a cluster of buildings. They were ahead of the Patternists and farther inland, away from the trail. Roofless and half demolished as they were, they could provide shelter.

The shooting had died down a little now. Most of it seemed to come from behind them, where there were hills and trees for cover. Most of the land before them now was flat and empty, covered only by tall, slowly dying grass and an occasional tree. The territory around Forsyth was semiarid. Redhill was lush and green all year, but now, in late spring, this land was turning brown.

A few yards away from the Patternists on one side was a sheer drop of about five meters. Beyond that was a slender ribbon of sand, and the ocean. The Clayarks could not shoot from that direction. In front of the Patternists and to their other side there was little cover beyond the dying grass—and the buildings, of course. But they were definitely empty. It looked as though the Clayarks would have to wait until the Patternists turned inland toward Forsyth. Not until then would there be more hills—the low hills that surrounded the sector itself. Teray could feel a general relaxation in the group.

The shot caught everyone off guard. Coransee's horse stumbled and went down. Amber's horse reared, out of control for a second, and the next shot went through Amber's left hand. Teray, fearful that she would be shot again, ignored the fallen Coransee and whipped out in search of the sniper. He could not find the creature, but he did discover the place from which the Clayark probably had fired. It was a dark round hole in the ground. Teray traced it down with his perception and discovered beneath the ground a network of tunnels. Doubtless they were ancient mute structures, dangerous now, even partially collapsed. But obviously the Clayarks had found them usable.

Coransee's horse was dead, a bullet lodged in its brain. The Housemaster took Amber's horse and ordered Amber to ride with Teray. They rode only the short distance to the ruins, though. It was time for a rest stop, and Amber needed a protected place to repair her shattered hand. Teray needed a protected place too—to do what it was certainly time for him to do.

He sat down beside Amber on the grassy floor of the building shell. She had chosen a spot as far as she could get from the others and began to repair her hand. Her injury bothered him because healing it would leave her weakened. She had to be strong if she was to have any chance of finishing Coransee—if he left Coransee in need of finishing. On the other hand, he could not tell her to get ready, that he was about to attack. Not while there was still the possibility, however slim, of surprising Coransee.

If she had been still linked with him, she would already know, and her emotional reaction would alert Coransee—and the fighting might already be over.

"I came over here to avoid spoiling anybody's lunch," she told him. "You won't like this either, but stay anyway."

"Won't like what?"

She opened her mouth as though to answer, but instead made a kind of wordless exclamation. "There," she said.

Teray's eyes were drawn automatically to her wounded hand where it lay in her lap, covered by her other hand. He looked at it, then back up at her quickly, in surprise.

"What did you do?" It was a foolish question. He could see what she had done. Her left wrist now ended in a smooth pale cap of new flesh. The thing that had been her left hand lay shriveled, detached in her lap.

"It was ruined," she said. "I had it doubled into a fist when the Clayark fired, and the bullet hit at just the right angle to destroy it." She held up the severed hand. It was literally nothing more than dried skin and bone—a claw. A misshapen claw with at least three of the fingers held on only by shreds of dried flesh.

"Looks like something mummified," said Teray.

"I took everything I could use from it before I shed it. I'll have another fully regenerated in about a month. If . . ." She shrugged.

If she lived another month. He was grateful to her for not finishing. "So long?" he asked quietly.

"It won't be that long. Not when you consider that it's not the only thing I'm growing." She smiled slightly.

He did not return her smile. He found himself staring at

the smooth, new cap of skin. It was easier to try to figure out how she had done such a thing than it was to think about the things she kept saying. "I'll get you something to eat when it's ready," he told her. He wanted her to eat and be as strong as she could. Coransee's people had located and lured in several wild rabbits. They were preparing now to roast them.

"That's all right," she said. "I'm not very hungry. In effect, I just ate my hand."

He grimaced, both repelled and pleased. However she had managed it, she had kept her strength. She could fight.

She looked at him silently for several seconds, then looked away. "You have an edge," she said quietly. "You're a latent healer. I'm sure of that now. Your teachers were either completely incompetent or too far from you in the Pattern to be able to work effectively with you. Or maybe they were just afraid of all that raw new strength that you could have accidentally killed them with."

"Wait a minute," he said. "What are you talking—"

"I don't have time to say it slowly, Teray. You're untrained so I don't know how much good your talent will do you. But he has almost no healing ability. You saw how he killed the Clayarks?"

"Yes, but . . ."

"What you learned easily, he can't learn at all. He's tried."

"Amber . . ."

"I'm sorry. I couldn't help realizing that you were about to go after him. And of course, he knew the moment I did. He's coming now."

Her last words echoed Iray's months before, when he had fought Coransee for the first time. He looked around, concealing sudden fear, and saw Coransee striding toward him. He spoke to Amber quietly. "All right, it doesn't matter. But you get out of here. Wait your turn."

"I don't want a turn."

He touched her face. "I'll try to see to it."

She left, glaring at Coransee as she passed him. She was with her ten guards before they realized that they were on duty.

"I thought you'd be ready sometime today," Coransee told Teray.

Teray considered getting up to face him, then rejected the idea. If he stood, he would have to waste part of his attention keeping his feet. He leaned back against the building wall. He was tightly shielded, as ready as he could be.

"Did you really expect Rayal to help you?" asked Coransee softly.

Teray held his face expressionless. He was almost used to Coransee invading his mental privacy by now. "If you knew I had called him, why didn't you attack?"

"Why should I have? Only someone who had spent all but the last few months of his life in school would believe he could get help by calling on Rayal."

Teray hit him.

The blow, not one of Teray's hardest, bounced off Coransee's shield. Teray struck again, testing the strength of the shield. It was like pounding with his fists against a stone wall. He remembered with longing the muteherd Jackman's eggshell shield.

Coransee hit back, rammed Teray's shield, not testing

but trying at once to demolish. Teray's shield withstood the blow.

Teray realized already that neither he nor Coransee would be pounded into defeat in the usual way. Something more was needed.

Teray swept his perception through Coransee's brain as though through the brain of a Clayark.

For an instant, Coransee frowned, seemed disoriented. But he was recovering himself even as Teray swept again. Somehow he deflected Teray's second sweep. Then abruptly he struck back.

As quick as Teray's sweep had been, the Housemaster almost caught him unshielded. And that deflection . . .

Safely shielded, Teray tried to understand what had happened. It was as though he had tried to land a physical blow and had had the blow blocked by his opponent's arm. It was not like running against the solid wall of a shield. No Patternist could lay a mind shield around his physical body. But apparently a strong Patternist could strike out with part of his strength to deflect attacks against his body. An attack that could be sensed could at the same time be deflected. Teray thought he understood. A second later Coransee tested his understanding.

Coransee struck at Teray's head. For a confused instant, Teray thought he perceived a physical object flying at him. A fraction later, he knew what it was, and used his new knowledge with fear-inspired accuracy.

Without understanding quite how he knew, Teray realized that he had just avoided—or at least postponed—a cerebral hemorrhage. Coransee was unwittingly teaching him to defend himself. If only he could learn fast enough.

Teray contracted the muscles of Coransee's legs savagely.

Before Coransee could stop himself, he fell screaming to the ground. He had been too busy guarding the vital parts of his body. He had not realized what agony his legs could give him.

And before he could shut that agony out, Teray hit him again—hit at what had to be a weakened, unattended shield.

And smashed through! He had a foothold.

Instantly Coransee forgot his legs and slashed at Teray.

Teray hit back hard, hit again and again. He was a man in armor battering a naked man. He had won. Surely he had . . . .

Coransee slammed him back, hammered at him as no shieldless Patternist should have been able to. Teray fought with savage desperation, unable to believe what was happening. The naked man was beating him into semiconsciousness.

Finally, Coransee tore Teray loose from his hard-won foothold. Tore him loose, held him, and continued to batter him. There was no longer any question. Coransee was stronger.

The Housemaster broke through what was left of Teray's shield and began beating Teray in earnest. Now Teray was the naked man.

Pain.

Teray could not think. He was ablaze with agony. He lashed out blindly. The old way of killing Clayarks—Coransee's way: the large artery just where it emerged from the heart.

Coransee had been foolish enough to relax his defenses. After all, he was winning.

For all his speed, he could not reestablish them in time. Teray ruptured the great blood vessel.

Coransee's attack collapsed. But even as he lay on the ground clutching his chest, trying to prevent himself from bleeding to death, he took his revenge.

Teray found himself suddenly disoriented. His head hurt. His head was exploding. He tried to reach up, clutching it between his hands. One of his arms would not work. He was going to be sick. He managed to turn his head so that he did not vomit over his own inert body. His mind was still working, still aware. In spite of the broken blood vessel in his brain, he was still conscious. He could still fight.

With his last strength, Teray swept through the struggling Housemaster's brain. Coransee had no defense now. He was completely occupied with his injury. Teray swept over him again and again, leaving himself no strength to keep his own body alive. He was killing both Coransee and himself, but his awareness had deteriorated to such a degree that he did not realize it. He realized only that he could not hold on to consciousness much longer. That he must do as much damage as he could while he could.

He did not know when Coransee's body went into violent convulsions. He did not know when Coransee's muscles contracted so violently that they snapped one of the Housemaster's legs. He did not know when Coransee bit off a large piece of his own tongue. He knew nothing until just before he lost consciousness completely. Only then did he realize that he had won. Coransee was dead.

Teray opened his eyes to a vast expanse of clear blue sky. It took him a moment to see the ragged walls of the ruin and realize where he was. He was weak and tired and ravenously hungry. He tried to remember what had happened.

Then it came back to him and he sat up abruptly. Too abruptly. He would have fallen back had Amber not been there to help him. She had come from nowhere, kneeling beside him, steadying him.

"It's over. You're all right. Eat."

There was food. Roast meat from somewhere. He stared at it. "What . . . ?"

"Rabbit, remember? We are as encircled by wild rabbits as we are by Clayarks."

He had been out for a while, then. They had had time to cook. That was to be expected. Coransee had all but killed him. He flexed his right arm—the one that hadn't worked the last time he had tried to use it—and moved his right leg. Both moved easily. Satisfied, he settled down to eating roast rabbit and fresh biscuits and drinking a great deal of water. He ate in silence for several minutes, concentrating only on the food. Finally, he spoke. "He is dead, isn't he?"

"Of course."

"He earned it."

She said nothing.

"I should be dead too. You saved me."

"Healed you."

"Did the others give you any trouble?"

"Not after they saw that he was dead. Two or three of them wanted to stop me from helping you but I convinced them not to."

He raised an eyebrow questioningly.

"They're still alive. They're probably going to give you trouble."

"I can handle them now that Coransee is dead." He looked around for Coransee's body. She read his glance and pointed past the clusters of waiting outsiders and women. Just beyond a ragged edge of wall, he could see two outsiders working at something, digging a hole, a grave.

"No," he said quietly.

Amber looked at him.

"The Clayarks will be at the grave the moment we leave. He's freshly killed. They'll gut him and eat him the way we did those rabbits. I'm not going to give any Patternist to them."

"What, then?"

"Burn him. Burn him to ashes." He looked at her. "Can you see that it's done thoroughly? Are you strong enough after your hand?"

She nodded.

The Patternists had gotten wood for their cooking fire from a pair of ancient dead trees behind the ruin. Now they took more of the wood, and made a funeral pyre for the fallen Housemaster.

The woman, Rain, had washed smeared blood from Coransee's face and closed his eyes. She had straightened his body on its pyre and wept over him. Now, as he burned, as Amber saw to it that he was completely incinerated, others wept too. Teray watched them impassively for a few moments, then walked away. There was something missing. He had hated Coransee. He had never been more pleased at another person's death. Yet . . .

The mutes would have made a ceremony, a funeral.

Mutes were ceremony-making creatures. Patternists had left such things to them for so long that there were almost no Patternist ceremonies left. For a funeral, ancient words would have been said, and the body consigned to the earth with quiet dignity. Even Patternists who thought no more of mutes than they did of draft animals attended such ceremonies with respect. They had become the due of any Patternist or mute who died—a time for friends, husbands, and wives to pay last respects. The ten who had belonged to Coransee, who now belonged to Teray, would have appreciated it.

Amber came to stand beside Teray. "It's done."

"All right."

"What are you going to do?"

"Get us out of here as soon as they've buried the ashes."

"While you were unconscious, they asked me which of us would lead them—you or me."

Teray turned to look at her, his expression cautious, questioning.

She smiled. "Would I have saved you if I wanted them that badly? You know they're yours. His whole House is yours."

"Did you . . . did you want it at all?"

"A House like that? If you had been anyone else, Teray, you and Coransee would have burned together."

He shuddered, knowing she meant it, knowing that he was alive only because she loved him. Not for the first time, he realized what a really dangerous woman she could be. If he could not make her his wife, he would be wise to make her at least an ally.

"I'd give you that House if it weren't so far from Forsyth," he said.

She raised an eyebrow.

"I don't want you that far away from me if I succeed Rayal."

"I think you will succeed him, but . . ."

"If I do, it will probably be in spite of whatever Rayal can do to stop me. But look, if it happens, I'll try to find a Housemaster in Forsyth who's willing to make a trade—move to Redhill. If I can't, I'll give you any help you need to establish a new House in Forsyth."

"You've decided I'm going to settle in Forsyth."

"At the very least, you're going to stay in Forsyth. After all, I'm offering you a bribe."

She laughed, as he had intended her to, but did not give him an answer, exactly. "Do you realize we're linked again?" she asked.

That startled him. He could see at once that it was true, but he had not been aware of linking with her. He could not recall when it had happened.

"I was healing you," she said. "I wasn't shielded, of course, and you just caught hold."

"I don't remember."

"You didn't know what you were doing. You were just returning to a familiar position. I didn't mind. Frankly, I was glad to have you back. If you wind up in Forsyth, one way or another, I'll get a House there."

He kissed her. She had put him in just the right frame of mind for the other thing he had to do. He went over to the cluster of outsiders and women who stood watching as

Coransee's ashes were covered with earth. When that was done, he spoke to them.

"Come back into the building and sit down," he told them. "We have one more thing to do before we go on."

They obeyed silently. Some of them, Rain in particular, clearly resented him, but they had seen him kill their Housemaster in a fair fight. Custom said they should lower their heads and accept him as their new Housemaster, unless one of them wanted to challenge.

"We're surrounded by Clayarks," he said. "If we go on through them the way we have, someone will be killed. Instead, I intend to kill the Clayarks. All of them. Now." The ten Patternists understood him. They began to look apprehensive. "I need your strength as well as my own for this," he continued. "I want all of you to open and link with me."

Immediately there was protest.

"You don't have any right to ask that of us," said a man named Isaac. "Even if we could be sure you knew what you were doing, that would be too much."

Teray said nothing, just looked at the man.

"We hardly know you, and you're asking us to trust you with our lives."

"Your lives will be safe with me."

"You say. Even Coransee never asked this of us."

"I'm not asking it either."

Isaac glared at him for a moment, then glanced out to where the ashes of Coransee were buried. Finally he lowered his head.

"Lord." It was Goran who spoke. There was no hostility in his voice. "Lord, we are all far apart in the Pattern.

196

Are you certain that anyone other than Rayal *can* bring us all together?"

"I can." He was surprised to realize that he actually was as confident as he sounded. He had never gathered such a widespread group before, yet he had no doubt that he could do it, or that he should do it. "Open to me," he said. "It will be easier on you if . . ."

"You don't know what you're talking about!" Rain. Teray had expected to have trouble with her. "You think you can do what he could because you're his brother? You think you're as good as he was?" She was standing up now, and shouting. Teray spoke to her quietly.

"Sit down, Rain, and be quiet."

"You're nothing compared to him, and you never will . . ."

She was much stronger than Jackman, but getting through her shield was not too difficult. Very carefully, he pushed her into unconsciousness—that to prevent her from wasting her strength fighting him. He formed a link with her. The unity was not pleasant even while she was unconscious, but he would get used to it.

"I understand her problem," he told the others. "I realize that some of the rest of you feel the same way. That's why I've been patient. But now I'm through being patient. Those of you who refuse to open, I will force—not necessarily as gently as I forced Rain. Goran?" He had chosen Goran because he knew the young outsider would not refuse.

Goran opened. Beside him, taking her cue from him, Lias also opened. That got things started. It was not necessary for Teray to force anyone else.

Within seconds, he controlled the combined strength of ten Patternists. He had linked, then taken from all ten at once. The exhilaration he felt was something totally new to him. The canopy of his awareness first seemed almost as broad as the sky itself.

Feeling like some huge bird, he projected his awareness over the territory. He could see, could sense, the lightly wooded land dotted with ruined buildings. He could see the distant ranges of hills, was aware of the even-more-distant mountains. The mountains were far beyond his striking range. In fact, they were near Forsyth, still over a day's journey away, but he could see them. He swooped about, letting his extended awareness range free through the hills and valleys. Then, finally, he settled down, and focused his awareness on the Clayarks who formed a wide half-circle around his party. He swept down on them, killing.

Before, with Amber, he had killed dozens of Clayarks. Now he killed hundreds, perhaps thousands. He killed until he could find no more Clayarks over all his wide range. He even checked the system of underground tunnels. When he was finished, he was certain that there were no more Clayarks anywhere near enough to affect him or his party.

Then suddenly Rayal was with him.

You've done well, young one. Very well. But be careful when you let your people go. Release only their strength. Keep your links with them.

What am I being careful of? he asked coldly. *You or my people?* He would never forgive the old man for refusing

198

him help when he needed it so desperately. Rayal picked up his thought.

I don't care whether or not you forgive me, young one. But keep in mind what you told Coransee's people a few minutes ago. I suspect I'm even less patient than you are.

Teray took the hint. *What do you want of me?*

Let the woman know that you'll be unconscious for a while once you let go of your people's strength. Tell her not to try to help you—just to keep your people off you. She did it once. She'll have to do it again. It's a good thing you hadn't taken from her too.

He had not taken strength from Amber because she had obviously been tired. She had done her share for the day, he had thought. Now, obediently, he relayed Rayal's thought to her. Rayal continued before she could reply.

Now let them go. All at once, the way you took them. If you try it one at a time, you might kill the last ones by giving back too much to the first one.

Teray obeyed, let the strength of the ten Patternists snap away from him like a released spring.

The breath seemed to go out of his body. There seemed to be nothing left of him. He sagged, the strength of his muscles gone. The strength of his mind kept him alive, but it did nothing more. He could still understand Rayal's mental voice speaking inside him, but it would be a while before he could respond.

Its never easy, sent the old man. *But the first time is always the worst. Ten or ten thousand, it doesn't make any difference if they aren't compatible with you. You pay for the power you take from them. You pay whether you take it through a few temporary links or through the Pattern itself.*

Can you tell whether the others are all right? Teray could not project the thought. He had no strength for that. But he hoped Rayal would pick it up.

They're fine. Even the one you had to knock out is still all right. They wonder what's the matter with you.

They aren't the only ones.

Rayal projected amusement. *You're fine. Recovering faster than I expected. You'd better be fine. I've stayed alive fifteen damnable years longer than I wanted to, waiting for you.*

In his surprise, Teray could not form a coherent thought.

Surprised, young one? It doesn't matter. As long as you're good enough to succeed me, nothing else matters.

But why would you wait for me? You had chosen Coransee.

Coransee had chosen himself.

But he said . . .

That's right. He said. Of course, he could have succeeded me. No doubt he would have if you hadn't killed him.

But you didn't want him to?

He wasn't good enough, young one.

He was stronger than I am.

That's not surprising. He was stronger than I would be alone—though I never let him know it. But the strength was all he had. That healing ability that your Amber found in you was all but missing in him. She's not the only healer who's tried to teach him.

But why would healing ability be that important to a Patternmaster?

The healing part of it isn't. It's the way a healer can

kill. The way Amber taught you. Without that method just now, you would have killed at least three of the people you just took power from. Three out of ten. You would have been punching holes in Clayarks, wasting strength that wasn't yours to waste. Imagine killing thirty per cent of the Patternists in even an average-size House.

Teray winced away from the idea. *Why didn't you tell me? Why didn't you tell him? If he understood, he might not have had to die.*

I wouldn't have sacrificed one of Jansee's sons if he hadn't had to die. Do you really think anyone could have talked him out of wanting the Pattern?

You could have, perhaps.

Young one, me least of all. Think! The only thing that kept him from attacking me outright to take the Pattern was the belief that it would come to him without a struggle if he waited a little longer.

Could he have taken it?

Very possibly.

Teray sighed, feeling the strength flowing back into his body. He could have opened his eyes if he had wanted to and seen Amber next to him waiting.

I will never gather the strength of the Pattern in my mind again, sent Rayal. *It would kill me. When the need arises next, young one, the Pattern will be yours. That will kill me, too, but at least I'll die alone—not take thousands of people with me.*

But you can't just give it to me. Others will contest . . . .

I will give it to you. You'd win it anyway. if there was anyone better than you around, I wouldn't have chosen you. And once you have it, with your health and strength, those who contest will be no more to you than that girl Rain. Remember that and treat them gently. Your only real opponent is dead.

But another healer . . . a better healer . . .

You've got a better healer sitting next to you. And she'll always be a better healer. You won't ever surpass her in healing skill. And she won't ever surpass you in strength. There are plenty of better healers, but no stronger healers. And no weaker healer could survive what you just survived. You have the right combination of abilities.

Teray sighed, opened his eyes, and sat up. He looked at Amber and she nodded slightly.

"I'm receiving too," she said. "He wants me to know."

Teray addressed Rayal. *You couldn't have kept Coransee from killing me, could you?*

No. Not unless I fought him. He had already made up his mind about you—and from his point of view, he was right. You were definitely a danger to him even though at first you didn't want to be. I didn't dare fight him. There was too much chance of his winning. So it was all up to you.

And you couldn't very well tell me without taking the chance of also telling him. Teray shook his head. *You've been bluffing everyone for a long time, Lord.*

Only for the past couple of years. Only since I've become so weak and sick that taking strength from any but the most compatible of my people would have killed me.

Still a long time to bluff people who might have read any slip in your thoughts.

A long, wearying time, the old man agreed. *Hurry and get here. You have no idea how tired I am.*

ABOUT THE AUTHOR

I'm a 46-year-old writer who can remember being a 10-year-old writer and who expects someday to be an 80-year-old writer. I'm also comfortably asocial—a hermit in the middle of Los Angeles—a pessimist if I'm not careful, a feminist, a Black, a former Baptist, an oil-and-water combination of ambition, laziness, insecurity, certainty, and drive.

I've had ten novels published so far: *Patternmaster*, *Mind of my Mind*, *Survivor*, *Kindred*, *Wild Seed*, *Clay's Ark*, *Dawn*, *Adulthood Rites*, *Imago*, and *Parable of the Sower*. I've also had short stories published in anthologies and magazines. One, "Speech Sounds," won a Hugo Award as best short story of 1984. Another, "Bloodchild," won both the 1985 Hugo and the 1984 Nebula awards as best novelette.

—**Octavia E. Butler**

**DON'T MISS THESE SCIENCE FICTION
MASTERPIECES FROM HUGO AND
NEBULA AWARD-WINNER**

OCTAVIA E. BUTLER

☐ **ADULTHOOD RITES**
  (C 145-20-903-8, $5.99 USA) ($6.99 Can.)
☐ **DAWN**
  (0-445-20-779-5, $5.50 USA) ($6.99 Can.)
☐ **IMAGO**
  (0-445-36-454-1, $5.50 USA) ($6.99 Can.)
☐ **MIND OF MY MIND**
  (0-446-36-188-7, $5.50 USA) ($6.99 Can.)
☐ **PARABLE OF THE SOWER**
  (0-446-60-157-7, $5.99 USA) ($6.99 Can.)
☐ **PATTERNMASTER**
  (0-446-36-281-6, $5.50 USA) ($6.99 Can.)
☐ **WILD SEED**
  (0-445-20-537-7, $5.99 USA) ($6.99 Can.)

WITHDRAWN
Monroe Coll Library

AVAILABLE AT A BOOKSTORE NEAR YOU FROM

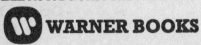 **WARNER BOOKS**

622-c